✳ BREEDING TIME ✳

The lush Danford farm in Tennessee was famous for the horses it bred—beautiful animals famous from coast to coast.

No stallion mounted a mare on the farm without the most careful calculations—but human mating habits were not as carefully regulated.

In the balmy Tennessee spring, and in the burning heat of the summer, anything could happen when a man and woman stood face to face . . .

"The confrontations of the races . . . untamed passions of hate and love . . . conflicts as elemental as those of an ancient Greek drama . . . Erskine Caldwell is as fresh and vivid as ever."
St. Louis Globe Democrat

Erskine Caldwell

The
Weather Shelter

A SIGNET BOOK from
NEW AMERICAN LIBRARY
TIMES MIRROR

Library of Congress Catalog Card Number: 73-83376

This is an authorized reprint of a hardcover edition published by The New American Library, Inc., in association with The World Publishing Company.

 SIGNET TRADEMARK REG. U.S. PAT. OFF. AND FOREIGN COUNTRIES
REGISTERED TRADEMARK—MARCA REGISTRADA
HECHO EN CHICAGO, U.S.A.

SIGNET, SIGNET CLASSICS, MENTOR AND PLUME BOOKS
are published by The New American Library, Inc.,
1301 Avenue of the Americas, New York, New York 10019

FIRST PRINTING, AUGUST, 1970

For Virginia

Chapter

ONE

The Danford pony breeding and schooling farm where Shetlands had been raised by father and son during the past forty years was several hundred acres of gently rolling foothills and fertile bottomland close to what people in the region for many generations had called the western rim of the bluegrass plateau.

The location of the extensive Danford estate was not far from the bend of the river where it turned abruptly along its course below the rocky rim of the highland and then followed a meandering lowland course through fields and forests. It was the only livestock farm of its kind in Wolver County even though there were numerous dairy herds in that region of abundant grazing land.

There were no large cities nearer than Nashville and Memphis, although Jackson at the time was rapidly increasing in size as many disheartened people in that part of the country abandoned uprofitable crop farms with the hope of being able to make a better living in the city, and the closest town, which was Wolverton, was only a little more than a mile from the Danford estate.

During the past forty years there had been little change in Wolverton's population of about a thousand white persons and almost as many Negroes. As some people had said when explaining why Wolverton's population had remained about the same for so long a time, if you left Wolverton to live somewhere else, you'd always feel too far away from home for comfort and would soon have to come back, and if somebody moved there to live, it wouldn't be long till he had to be straitjacketed and carried off to the insane asylum.

Wolverton was where some of the people lived who worked for Grover Danford at the pony farm or who had worked for Grover's father many years before and were now retired. Most of the other people living there owned small crop farms nearby or had jobs at the stock-feed milling and bagging works or in the large butter and cheese plant.

The principal business section of Wolverton was only three blocks long. The bank and the post office were at the eastern end of Union Street, situated on opposite corners, and the big brick Baptist and Methodist churches with tall white steeples were on corners at the western end. In the center of town stood the square-set gray-stone Wolver County courthouse topped by its ancient belfry and the highest pigeon roost in Wolverton. In addition to a drugstore, a poolroom, a fish market, and the Crystal Palace Cafe, along the three business blocks of Union Street were numerous small grocery, hardware, family clothing, and variety stores.

Down by the railroad tracks in the Negro district of unpaved streets and wooden shacks and tarpaper shanties, which the people who lived there called Halfway Hollow because they said it was a place where you could get so hungry you would feel half dead and half alive, there were several unpainted frame churches, a dilapidated six-grade public school, a smoldering trash dump, and a few ma-and-pa grocery and meat stores.

The town's elite residential district of white homeowners was a pleasant neighborhood situated high above Halfway Hollow with modern brick and stucco houses, well-tended lawns and shrubbery, and paved sidewalks and streets where prosperous lawyers, doctors, merchants, and a few wealthy widows had their homes and gardens.

Closely settled and mostly a one-story town of dwellings for both rich and poor, Wolverton had been built on the slope at the rim of the bluegrass plateau, and almost everybody living there was within sight of the miles and miles of gleaming white four-panel board fencing that completely surrounded the Danford pony farm and criss-crossed the numerous pastures, hay fields, feeding lots, and training paddocks. In the center of the estate stood the hilltop Danford mansion, an imposing landmark for nearly half a century, and slightly below the gabled white mansion was the orderly cluster of stables and barns.

Varying in color from sorrel and roan and chestnut to flashy buckskin and dappled gray, the blond-mane, long-tail, young Shetlands were often sold in lots of ten, fifteen, or more at a time to commission brokers and shipped by train or truck to retail livestock dealers as far away as Chicago and Boston. However, frequently sales were made in smaller numbers to operators of pony-ride concessions at fairs and carnivals and amusement parks in various parts of the country.

There had been a consistently good market for the

8

Danford ponies year after year, and buyers, especially the pony-ride operators who were concerned about injuries to young children and resulting lawsuits and who wanted well-trained and gentle Shetlands, willingly paid the asking prices. And almost every year some animal trainers came to select several of the Danford-bred colts to be taken away and trained to perform in circus acts with dogs and monkeys and clowns.

The most pleasing sale of all, however, was when parents brought a small child to the farm to select a pony of his own. When this happened, the foreman and stable boys alike were not always dry-eyed when they gave the pony a farewell pat on the rump. And as for Grover Danford himself, always moved by the excitement and yearning of a small boy or girl, he would practically give the pony away at a time like that.

The foreman, Jim Whittaker, and the stable boys would swear that every big saddle horse and stallion on the farm would whinny and stomp the ground every time a young pony was haltered and led up a trailer ramp to be taken away to live in some distant part of the country.

The spirited saddle horses, looking awesome in size beside the tiny Shetlands, were the ones that Grover and Jim Whittaker rode when they went off to inspect the fencing and nail down loose boarding or when herding the mares and foals from pastures to paddocks. There was very little other work for the big horses in the warm months of the year. However, there were many times in the winter months when the horses had to be hurriedly saddled, sometimes even in the middle of the night, to round up the Shetlands and drive them to the cover of the stables when there was an unexpected change in the weather and danger of an immediate sleet or snow storm.

II

Grover Danford, a tall, thickset, brown-haired, friendly-mannered man, and the sole owner of the pony farm by inheritance, was in his late thirties when at last he married after several years of loneliness following the death of Kathlee.

After the marriage, Grover and his wife, Madge, lived in the many-roomed, three-storied white mansion that had been built by his father on the highest ridge of the estate. Among the first demands Madge had made as soon as they were married was to have an expensive automobile of her own, and it had to be a sporty convertible and

9

painted in a particular shade of red which she herself was to select.

Grover was deeply in love with Madge and eagerly gave her anything she wanted. In addition to the red convertible, she said she wanted him to open unlimited charge accounts at several Nashville stores for her and to give her on the first day of every month an allowance, the amount of which she would determine from time to time.

He had known Madge only a short time before they were married. They had met at an alumni dance and house party following a football game at the university in Knoxville and, after Madge's forthright suggestion when she found out that he was far from being poor, the wedding took place a few weeks later at the home of her parents in Nashville. Even though he had tried to be patient and considerate ever since, Grover could not keep from becoming increasingly disturbed and wondering if she really loved him enough to be his wife.

For one thing, Madge had not only refused to go away on a honeymoon trip to New Orleans or Miami Beach, or anywhere else, her excuse being that she was unable to leave because she was undergoing important treatment by a Nashville doctor that could not be interrupted, but also she had firmly ruled that there was to be no customary first night of marriage at home for the same reason. She had slept in a separate bedroom ever since and it was all the more frustrating to Grover because she had always managed to have an excuse not to sleep with him even before they were married. Sometimes she said she had a bad cold or a splitting headache, or her excuse would be that she had a painful soreness in her back or some other incapacitating physical ailment.

Blondly beautiful, slender, vivacious, delicately feminine in appearance, and still in her late twenties, Madge Danford frequently became restless and quickly angered and would loudly complain that she was bored at home without the parties and luncheons and other social life of the city. It soon became a habit for her to leave home, often without a word spoken to Grover and sometimes even in the middle of the night, and drive her fiery red car to Nashville where she would stay for a week or longer at a time.

Once at midnight Grover had followed Madge from the house to the driveway when she was going to leave for Nashville.

"Please don't do this, Madge," he pleaded with her as he stood at the door of her car. She had already started the

10

engine and was racing it loudly. "Don't go off like this, Madge. Don't leave me. Stay here with me."

Tilting her head backward, she laughed at him.

"Me! Me! Me! That's all you care about! Yourself! Me! Me! Me!"

"But I don't want you to go off alone like this in the middle of the night, Madge. It's not safe. Listen to me. Something could happen to you along the road at this time of night. Wait until morning, anyway. Please, Madge."

"I know! You think you can keep me here if you scare me enough, and I might come crawling into bed with you!"

"Of course I want you to do that, Madge. Don't you ever want to? Don't you intend to? After all this time? When I asked you to marry me—"

She laughed at him again. "Is that what you wanted me to marry you for?"

"Well, that's part of it, Madge. I love you and—"

"If you feel so sorry for yourself, I'll help you out, Grover. I'll tell you what to do about it. Go on back in the house and get in your bed. Then pull up the covers and shut your eyes and go to sleep and maybe you'll have a long sweet dream about it."

With a wave of her hand and a roar of the engine, she drove away into the night. She did not come back home that time for more than a week.

III

Grover had had an elaborate wickerwork governess cart made in Kentucky especially for Madge soon after they were married and had told her that he wanted her to select any pony on the farm to be her own. Also, that was when he explained that the pony cart had been purposely made sturdy and roomy so that she could take one or two small children riding with her. As usual, Madge had laughed at him for intimating that he wanted her to have children and told him that riding around in a pony cart was a simpleminded country kind of thing to do and that she would be a lot happier going to parties and playing bridge with her friends in Nashville.

The handsome pony cart, still not used even once after all that time, was kept polished and shiny under a canopy in a stall of its own in one of the barns. Always hopeful that Madge would change her mind, Grover saw to it that the axles were kept greased and that there was never a speck of rust to be found anywhere on the cart. And

11

whenever he looked at it and imagined he could see Madge and their children riding around the ring, he always recalled the one time in their lives when he thought Madge was at last going to relent and let him make love to her.

It had happened on a warm summer evening while they were walking in the flower garden. They had left the house after supper and gone out into the twilight as the street-lights of Wolverton below began twinkling in the balmy night. He had never been able to remember what they had been talking about in the beginning, but he knew he would never forget the way Madge suddenly put her arms around his neck and kissed him excitedly with the full opening of her lips. It was the first time she had ever done anything like that and he wondered if a balmy summer night and a red rose could have impelled her to be affectionate and loving. What he had done a few moments before that was to take out his pocket knife and cut a long-stemmed red rose from one of the bushes. After carefully trimming the thorns from the stem, he handed it to her smilingly but without a word spoken. That was when she suddenly put her arms around him and kissed him so fervently.

He was holding her so close to him that he could feel the beating of her heart and then she began sobbing and pressed her cheek tightly against his face.

"Grover—Grover—" she murmured.

"What's the matter, Madge?" he asked. "Tell me. Why are you crying like this? What's wrong?"

She tightened her arms around his neck.

"I want so much to love you, Grover," she sobbed with a trembling of her body.

Feeling the warmth of her tears on his face, he stroked her comfortingly.

"We can love each other, Madge. That's the way it ought to be."

She held her breath for moment after moment.

"I do—I do—I want to so much, Grover," she said excitedly after that. "You don't know how much I want to love you—please believe me—you've got to believe me. Don't ever think anything else—no matter what happens. I can feel how much I love you—how much I really want to. I know it's there—I can feel it inside me. And that's what makes me cry—just thinking about it. But then I have to go away—I can't stay—I can't make myself stop doing that. I've cried about it ever since we were married—and I didn't want you to know I cried so much—I didn't want you to know about it. But you gave me this rose. And

12

then I couldn't help myself. It made me so happy for you to do that—I know you did it because you love me. I know it—I know it! But now I wish you hadn't done that. It makes me feel so sad. So miserable. And that's why I couldn't keep from crying about it. I'm so ashamed of myself. I wish—I wish—oh, if I could only be different—if only for just a little while—and not the way I am—that's what makes me so sad and miserable! Grover! Grover!"

"Don't talk like that, Madge," he said tenderly. "I want you to keep on knowing I love you so much—more than I can tell you. Now you can't feel sad and miserable, can you, Madge? Hasn't all that feeling gone away now? Please say you won't feel like that anymore."

There was a tense tightening of her body in his arms.

"Grover—"

"What is it, Madge?"

He could feel the warmth of her tear-wet cheeks pressing against his face.

"Don't hate me, Grover. Please don't. I can't help it. God knows that's the truth. I just can't help it. It's the way I am. If I could only love you the way I want to—the way you want me to—the way it ought to be! That's what I want—and I can't—I can't!"

"Don't worry about it like this, Madge," he told her soothingly. "Everything's going to be all right from now on. We'll see to that."

"No! No! It won't be—it can't be—and I can't help it!" she sobbed almost indistinctly. "It has to be the way it is—nothing can change it!"

He picked her up and carried her from the flower garden and across the wide veranda and into the house. Crying softly with her tear-wet face pressed tightly against his, she clung to him desperately while they were going through the lower hall and until they were at the top of the stairway. They were almost at her bedroom door when she suddenly screamed hysterically and clawed his face so painfully with her fingernails that he had to put her down.

As she ran to her bedroom door, he could feel the trickling of blood on his face and neck and he tried to wipe some of it away while he stood there bewildered and confused by her behavior.

"Please, Madge," he begged. "We've waited all this time. Don't make me wait any longer. I love you—you know I do—and I want you now, Madge!"

"Stay out of my room!" she had told him in a screaming cry of distress that was like that of a frightened child. "Leave me alone! Don't touch me! Don't come near me!"

"If I wait a little while, will you open the door for me then, Madge?"

"No! You can't do that! I won't let you find out! Never! Never!"

IV

Not a word had been said by either of them the next morning about what had taken place the night before and it had never been mentioned since. However, no matter how many times Grover had thought about what had happened, he was never able to think of a satisfactory explanation for Madge's hysterical outburst at her bedroom door so soon after hugging and kissing him so affectionately.

At first he had suspected that she was in love with another man, but when he finally asked her outright to tell him the truth, her denial was so emphatic and convincing that he no longer suspected her of being unfaithful. Ever since that night at her bedroom door he had been waiting patiently, and always hopefully, for her to give the slightest indication that she would no longer resist his lovemaking, and the saddest time of all was when she would suddenly go away on one of her frequent trips to Nashville.

Once when Madge left home in her sporty red convertible, and without even a wave of her hand to Grover as she drove away, Jim Whittaker watched her with a solemn shaking of his head until the roaring red automobile had disappeared from sight.

Jim, who was a little more that fifty years old at the time and had four sons and daughters who had married and left home, was a tall, lean, ruddy-faced horseman with light blue eyes and graying dark hair. After finishing the final year at the Wolverton white public school, which at that time was no higher than the seventh grade, Jim had gone to work as a stable boy at the age of thirteen for Grover's father, and he had known Grover since the morning of his birth in the big white mansion on the ridge. Ever since the day when Jim had carefully held him astride a pony for the first time, and showed him how to pat the pony's neck with one hand and keep the bridle reins clutched tightly in his other hand, everything Grover had learned about the breeding and training and care of the Shetlands had been taught to him over the years by Jim Whittaker.

"Grover," Jim had said as they stood at the paddock railing long after Madge's car had gone out of sight over

14

the highland rim that morning, and while both of them were still gazing at the winding road, "Grover, you still don't have a woman who acts like a wife to you after you've waited all this time to get married. It's a goddam shame and I don't like to see it the way it is. When a woman gets married, there's a special place for her, and that one you married ain't in it. This's no way for a woman to treat a man she's married to—going off to stay nobody knows how long and not ever bothering to look back at you when she left. It's a hateful thing for her to do to you. It sure ain't none of my personal business, and I'll be the first to admit it, but if you'd listen to me, boy, the next time you can catch her here at home you'd better grab her and pull up her dress and rip off her drawers and spank her contrary rump till it gets as red as the paint on that car she drives."

"Maybe she'll change before much longer, Jim."

"I don't see no signs of her getting ready to change her ways, boy. Maybe you do, but I sure don't. She goes off to Nashville or wherever it is she goes more and more all the time. And that ain't good. When a man gets his urge and wants his woman, and she's nowhere around for a whole week or so—"

"I waited this long—I can wait a little longer."

"I know you've been waiting. But how goddam long can a man hold on to himself and wait it out even if he was somehow sure he was going to get what he was waiting for? Let me tell you, boy. It ain't a human natural thing for a man to get married and then have to hold on to himself for God knows how long."

Shaking his head and saying nothing more, Grover turned around and walked toward the stable. Jim hesitated for a moment and then followed him from the railing.

"Go on and tell me to shut up about it if you want to, boy. But if you don't, I'm going to keep on worrying and complaining about it."

Grover still had said nothing more when Jim caught up with him.

"Well, I know why you'd want to marry her to start with, boy. I've seen enough of her prettiness to be goddam sure about that. She's as good-looking to look at as you can let your mind think about a young woman being. But why in the world did she marry you and then turn around and start acting contrary like she does? Was it just only to marry rich and spend your money and nothing else?"

"I don't know, Jim. I just don't know."

"Well, that's what worries me. Because it's you and I

can't help from being upset about it. Does she get female busy in the bed and make up good for everything the way a woman ought to for a man after she's gone and behaved herself contrary as all hell? I mean, when she's here and ain't off to hell-and-gone somewhere else like she is now for a week or more? If she don't do real extra good in bed when busyness counts the most—hell, boy, if she don't do that, goddam if any of them's worth a tin dime in a blind man's begging cup. I don't claim to be an expert about a lot of things—but when it comes to haltering a mare for a stallion to mount—"

Jim had followed Grover as far as the stable door and then went no farther when Grover went inside out of sight. Standing in the doorway, he waited expectantly for Grover to say something. After a long silence, Jim called to him.

"I don't know if you're hearing me in there."

"I can hear you, Jim."

"Well, there's one more thing—"

"What is it?" Grover asked.

"Maybe I oughtn't to—"

"Go on and say it."

"Well, I know it's none of my goddam business no more now than it ever was, boy, but I can't hold back and I've just got to say it anyhow."

There was a long pause while Grover waited to hear what Jim might say.

"I'm listening," Grover said presently.

"You've been married to her for better than two years now already, boy, and there's still no sign of some young ones up there in that great big house with all those empty rooms. That's not the way it ought to be, like I can't keep from thinking all the time. Every man wants a son of his own. It's a natural thing for a man to want—or he'll settle for a daughter to start with if he can't get the other first. And a son will come if you try enough times. Anyhow, you got born here for your daddy to pass this pony farm along to and you know you ought to have a son for the same reason. You don't want this fine place to go and get put up at auction when you're dead and have it end up owned by some goddam nobody who don't know a bellyband from a croupstrap. Hell, no! Now if I know the female branch as good as I think I do, when she comes back here from Nashville this time, you bring her down here to the breeding shed and I'll—"

"Wait a minute, Jim!" Grover called from the stable. "What are you talking about?"

"You wait. I'll finish what I was saying. You get her

16

down here to the breeding shed and I'll bring in Mr. Pepper or Showboy and the next mare we're going to breed, which is going to be either Gypsy Girlee or Lady Pauline. I'll look at the stud chart and get that all decided beforehand. Then you keep her here the whole time—even if you have to halter her with some ropes—and I'll bet you the best pair of boots in the store that she can't help herself from turning into a real female kind of woman after that. And it won't take her long, neither, if she's any part of female. I know what I'm saying, boy, because I still remember how my wife got female busy right after I took her to the breeding shed the first time. You do like I said and find out for yourself. There just ain't no better cure in the whole world than that for contrary female standoffishness."

TWO

The **Danford** breeding shed, stables, barns, and shops, all colorfully painted in a traditional shade of harvest red with glossy white trim and always looking freshly painted no matter how dark and gloomy the weather, had been built in a horseshoe-shaped cluster on a broad leveling of land east of the stately white mansion. In the center of it all, there were numerous paddocks, and farther away was the oval riding ring. West of the cluster of buildings, about two hundred yards away and situated far apart on both sides of the fast-running spring-fed brook called Saddle Creek, were a number of small white cottages where Jim Whittaker and Mike Devlin and some of the other married workers lived.

Close to the southern boundary of the white-fenced pony farm, and only a brief walk from the railroad tracks and about a half mile from the weatherworn frame dwellings in the Halfway Hollow district of Wolverton, there was a large freshwater pond always filled to the brim by several springs that never ran dry even in a severe summer drouth.

Also not far from the southern boundary, and within a hundred yards of the pond, there was a large foursquare shingle-roofed weather shelter that had been standing there for many years and was always amply stocked with a year's supply of freshly baled alfalfa and timothy. Three sides of the building were weatherboarded and whitewashed. The remaining side had been left unboarded to provide an ample opening for the ponies and, for the protection of excited colts galloping in and out, all squared timbers were well padded with burlap wrapping. And like all the other Danford buildings, the weather shelter had a lightning rod jutting high above the peaked roof.

The pond had become almost completely surrounded by a growth of young oak trees and willows and entwining honeysuckle vines and it had not been used for watering the Shetlands since a towering storage tank and a low row of water troughs had been installed closer to the stables and paddocks. However, the box-shaped weather shelter continued to be the favorite gathering place for every new generation of colts since it provided shade when the summer sun was hot and a roof when there was a drenching thunderstorm.

As had been the custom since the time when Grover's father, George Danford, began breeding and selling ponies, young boys in Wolverton, when they were nine or ten years old, both white and black, and if they weighed no more than seventy pounds to begin with, were hired and paid weekly wages to help train the young Shetlands to the halter first and then to take bridle and saddle without shying and bucking.

After the period of preliminary training, the boys rode in the paddocks and ring until the young Shetlands became accustomed to saddle and rider and were considered by Jim Whittaker to be sufficiently trained, or broke, as Jim would say, so that very young children could ride them safely. It was a sort of graduation ceremony for boy and pony when they were at last permitted to leave the paddocks and gallop as they pleased in one of the large pastures without the supervision of Jim Whittaker or anybody else. For a boy and his pony to have the freedom of a pasture for the first time was always an exciting event at the stables. And when the boy came back from the gallop, the other boys would gather around him enviously and watch him unsaddle the pony and wipe down the saddle sweat and groom the blond mane and long tail.

With the exception of a few, usually being boys who had a fear of being kicked or thrown and trampled by the colts, most of the young boys of Wolverton were always eager to help with the training and would gladly have worked without pay for the privilege. Some of the boys would cry and plead to be allowed to keep on riding the Shetlands when Jim Whittaker, after putting them on the jockey scales, had to tell them that they had reached the weight limit of eighty pounds, and explained that it would make a young pony swaybacked to carry any additional weight.

"Mr. Jim, please don't make me quit riding now," was a frequent plea of a weeping boy. "I only weigh a little bit more than I did last week. It's hardly none at all. You can look at me and see that, can't you? That little bit won't make much difference, will it, Mr. Jim?"

"I'm sorry, son," Jim would say. "I know how you feel about it but it can't be helped. That's the rule and it's what we go by. And you wouldn't want one of these fine ponies to have to be swaybacked or bowlegged all his life."

"But, Mr. Jim, if I come back next week and don't weigh too much then, can I ride again?"

"No, son. It's final. But maybe someday you can be a jockey and ride race horses."

"I don't want to ride a big horse—I want to ride a Shetland pony."

As it sometimes happened, complaining parents would come to the stables and blame Jim Whittaker because their son was starving himself and stunting his growth in an effort to keep his weight down so he could continue riding. Other parents had complained, and some had even become angry and abusive, when Jim Whittaker would not give a boy a riding job because he was excessively chubby and already overweight at the age of nine or ten. Whatever the complaint, though, Jim would say that it was his job to train and protect the ponies and not to raise somebody else's children.

And as for a boy who was no longer permitted to ride after he had been weighed on the jockey scales and had been told that he had reached the limit of weight, it was not unusual for him to come back to the stables time after time and sit forlornly on the paddock railing with tears streaming down his cheeks while he watched a younger and smaller boy stroke and saddle and then ride around the ring on his favorite pony. When he could no longer endure the anguish of it, he would go trudging homeward as if he had nothing more to live for.

When one of the boys, Jeff Bazemore, a Negro with exceptionally light coloring and wavy brown hair who was twelve years old at the time, suddenly shot upward in weight and height overnight, he was so tearful and heart-broken when he stepped from the jockey scales that Jim Whittaker even had to wipe tears from his own eyes. The quadroon boy, who in appearance was obviously second generation of racial mixture, had been helping with the training in the afternoon after school and every day in summer for the past three years. He knew so well the methods of handling the Shetlands, beside being so careful and considerate of them, that the foreman had been letting him give routine instruction and advice to the boys who came there to ride for the first time.

Jeff Bazemore lived in the Halfway Hollow section of Wolverton with foster parents, Mary and Pete Lawson, who had three children of their own about the same age as Jeff, and he considered himself to be an orphan. Pete

20

Lawson was handicapped, having lost a leg in a sawmill accident when he was a young man, and he received meager wages as a part-time janitor at the Wolver County courthouse. Pete's wife did washing and ironing in her house for several white families. And as for Jeff, he had always given the money he earned at the stables to his foster parents for his support—and Grover Danford had seen to it that his wages were considerably more than the other boys received. Jeff had been adopted and raised by the Lawsons and all he knew about his mother was that she had been a schoolteacher and was shot to death when he was a few months old.

The man who had killed Jeff's mother with two blasts of a shotgun was a Negro who claimed to be a barber but was actually engaged in activities outside the law and who had followed her from Memphis to Wolverton when he found out she was living there and teaching in the Negro school. Just before his mother died on the front porch of the Lawson house where she had boarded for nearly two years, she told Mary Lawson that the man who shot her had been trying for a long time to make her live with him in Memphis and give him the money she was to get from other men and this time he had said he was going to kill her if she still refused to do as she was told.

After his mother's death, letters from relatives who lived in Tupelo were found by the Lawsons in her room, but by then she had already been buried in the cemetery behind the African Methodist Episcopal Church in Wolverton. The adoption of Jeff by the Lawsons was approved at the courthouse soon after the burial, and when Pete Lawson asked the Negro undertaker about his bill, Pete was told that it had already been paid in full by somebody else.

Being much lighter in color than any of the other children in school and on the street where he lived, and having light brown hair that was wavy and not kinky, Jeff Bazemore had been teased since an early age by older boys and girls for not being black like they were and not having their kind of hair. He had never felt ashamed of being as he was, but he often wondered why he was not like the other children in Halfway Hollow.

After hearing one of the singsong chants of the older children many times, he finally asked Mary Lawson why they were teasing him like that.

Mary had heard the chanting, too, and all she could tell him was that his mother would be proud of his being as he was and for him never to regret it, for her sake. Jeff

21

had heard that particular chant so often that he was able to repeat every word of it.

> *Hey! Hey! Nigger boy! Nigger boy!*
> *Show me your face!*
> *I want to see your white daddy's*
> *New human race!*

"Mama Mary, why do they keep on saying that to me?" he had asked her. "I don't have a daddy—not a real daddy. I'm an orphan. You said so."

"Children have to make up something and behave like that, Jeff. But they don't always know what they're saying. Just pretend it's something they made up for no reason at all. They'll make up some others and forget all about that one."

"But why did they make that up about me?"

"Never mind, Jeff."

"Maybe I did have a white daddy, Mama Mary," he insisted. "I wasn't always an orphan, was I?"

"You wait till you grow up more to think about such things," she told him evasively. "You're too young now to worry about something like that. There'll be plenty of time later."

"When I grow up some more, Mama Mary, will you tell me then why I'm not black, but not all white either, so I'll know why I was born like I am?"

"If you don't find out all you want to know by the time you get to be a big boy, Jeff, then I'll tell you. But you've got to wait and grow up first."

As Jeff grew taller, and his quadroon color of skin became more noticeable even when he was with playmates of mulatto coloring, he was taunted more and more by the older boys and girls for being different and looking more like a white boy than a Negro. There was one particular chant that a group of older children living in the next block took delight in singing whenever he was sent on an errand to the grocery store at the corner.

> *Mama! Mama! Don't you tell me no lie!*
> *Why'd you make me a half-white bastard guy?*

Jeff had tried to ignore all the taunting chants until he heard one that made him so angry he got into several fistfights on the school playground. And because the children knew how angry it made him, he was soon hearing it wherever he went all summer long.

I have a little brother
With shiny brownish hair.
My mama says she got him
Out behind the county fair.
He can't grow black and kinky,
But that's not why he's mad.
He says he'll keep on pouting
Till he finds his whitey dad.

II

By the time Jeff was nine years old, he had stopped playing even with the three Lawson children at home, and soon after that he began going every day to the Danford stables. For the next three years, summer and winter, he spent every hour he could working with the Shetlands and learning from Jim Whittaker how to train and take care of the colts.

The afternoon when Jim Whittaker told Jeff that he was two pounds over the limit of weight and could no longer ride a pony, his eyes filled with tears and he could not say a word as he stepped from the jockey scales. Several younger boys were saddling ponies in the paddocks and another boy had already mounted his favorite pony and gone to the riding ring. He watched for a long time and then, wiping the tears from his eyes, he went back to the scales.

Jim Whittaker, knowing after years of experience that boys like Jeff Bazemore nearly always begged to be weighed a second time, was waiting at the scales for him.

"Mr. Jim, maybe there was something wrong," he said hopefully. "Would you weigh me again to be sure about it?"

Jim nodded. "Once more and that'll be all. But don't expect it to be no different this time."

His weight on the scales was exactly the same as it had been the first time.

"It had to happen sometime, Jeff," Jim told him consolingly. "It just couldn't be put off no longer. And so now you can start growing up into manhood. You won't be a little boy no more from now on."

Jeff walked away, his shoulders sagging with disappointment, as more tears came to his eyes. When he got to the paddock, he climbed to the top railing and sat there staring unseeingly at the younger boys with the ponies.

"Hey, Jeff!" one of the boys called to him. "What you

23

going to do when you can't ride a pony no more? You going to be a retired old man from now on?"

He pretended he had not heard a word of what was said.

"Don't go and get mad and run away from home, Jeff," another boy called to him.

Grover had been watching from the window of the stable office, well aware of what was happening, and he came outside then and walked over to the scales.

"Have you tested the scales lately, Jim?" he asked. "Are you sure about them?"

"I keep them true all the time, Grover. They're right on the dot like they ought to be. Couldn't nothing be wrong about them now."

Grover pointed at Jeff on the paddock railing.

"Then we're going to take on a new stable boy, Jim," he stated. "Starting right now. He's grown up enough for a bigger job and more pay. He's going to work here at the stables after school hours, on weekends, and every day in summer from now on."

"What for?" Jim spoke out immediately with a disapproving scowl. "Why do you say that, Grover? I don't need no more goddam help around here. Everything's going good just like it is. I've got plenty of stable help. I don't want to take him on or nobody else. I'm the foreman and I know what I need and what I don't need. When I need more help around here, you'll hear from me about it."

"I've got a reason for this, Jim," Grover told him calmly.

"What reason?"

"I want him to start learning all there is about what we do here."

"I don't have no spare time to waste doing that. It's not part of my job, anyhow."

"Then I want you to make it part of your job. The boy rode and trained colts for nearly three years and that was a good beginning for him. And so now I want you to teach him everything you know about breeding and handling ponies from start to finish. It would be a good idea first of all to teach him how we wean the foals the way we do with the correct mixture of molasses in their protein feed. Put him in charge of that to begin with. Then later he can work backward and forward from there and get to know the whole range of it."

"Why?" Jim demanded suspiciously. "What the hell for? I told you once already—"

"It's because I want him to grow up to be as much of an expert in this business as you are and help us improve the stock. Jeff's at the right age now to begin learning what I want him to know."

"I don't like hearing the way you say that, Grover," Jim protested roughly, even more displeased. "I'll be goddam if I'm going to bend over and learn him or nobody else to take my job away from me. I may not be too smart about some things but I'm not that much of a fool that way. I've worked with this Danford stock ever since your daddy hired me forty years ago when I was thirteen years old and I'm going to keep on doing it and can't nothing stop me. I'll still be the foreman around here twenty or more years from now, too."

"That's nothing for you to worry about, Jim. We don't even have to talk about that again. Forget it. You've got a lifetime job here."

Jim turned his head and glanced at Jeff sitting on the paddock railing.

"Well, if you want to know the truth, that ain't all that bothers me about it," he said after that.

"What else is it?"

"Now, I didn't bring this up. You started the whole thing yourself."

Grover nodded. "All right, Jim. I started it. Now you go ahead and say what else is bothering you."

"I'm a white man, Grover, goddam it. You know what that means. I was born white and I was raised white and I feel white and you can't be no more white than that. That's why I've got white man's principles and why I ain't changing them at my age. You couldn't be a white man yourself and fail to understand that about it, could you?"

"Go ahead, Jim. I'm listening."

"All right. I'll tell you what's bothering me. I get along fine with the colored people in this life as long as they want to work for me the way I tell them and watch their talk and stay in their place and act like the colored ought to. That's the reason I don't like it one bit to see one of them get moved up to my footing and treated like he's as white as I am. That's why it bothers me to see you pick out that Jeff Bazemore to be good to for no reason. You've been paying him double what the other young boys get for the same work and he says he takes it all down there and hands it over to Pete Lawson for his support because he's an orphan. If you want to be kind-hearted to him because of him being an orphan—well, that's your business and none of mine. But now you come

25

along and say you want to move him up so he'll stand right next to me where my footing is. That's different. I don't like that none at all."

"It can't be helped, Jim. That's the way it is."

"It don't have to be. Instead of pushing a colored boy along like that, you could be getting a son of your own—and a white one at that. That's what I keep on telling you. Your daddy did that for you and now it's your turn. That's family pride. You know you ought to have your own son to leave this pony farm to when you're gone so it'll be kept in the family like it ought to be. You've got a wife. And you ought to be a man enough to manage a woman. That's what a woman is for. What the hell, Grover! If I was married to a female who wouldn't stay at home and get in the goddam bed and raise kids for me and if—"

"In the meantime, Jim, you remember what we were talking about not long ago, don't you?"

"What was that?"

"That's when we both agreed it's time to introduce some strong new bloodlines and improve the breed of Danford ponies. We've got to keep up with the times. Pony racing and roadstering is catching on fast all over the country and we want to be in the running with our stock. We decided to do some crossbreeding with Welch and Indian pinto and maybe some Arabian bloodlines to get a little more size and speed and some good show points. I've decided that to start with we'll buy a young Welch stallion and then go on from there. I'm going up to Kentucky soon and look around to find out what's available now."

A wide smile came to Jim Whittaker's face.

"I like to hear you talk like that, Grover. It does me good to hear it because it's the smart thing to do. I'm all for it. We've got to keep on improving the Danford breed if we expect our stock to be first-rate enough to be proud of in the show-ring or out. I don't want to live to see Danford ponies get inbred and peter out to nothing but common third-rate scrub stock. I don't want to see my life wasted and come to that. I want a blue-ribbon breed and nothing else. That's why I'm in favor of doing some racing and roadster cross-breeding and getting started on it right away."

His smile suddenly vanished and he took several steps backward.

"But hold on now," he said, looking straight at Grover. "What's that got to do with a colored boy like Jeff Bazemore? You're mixing up two different things."

"If some good selective cross-breeding will improve the bloodlines of Danford ponies—"

"What kind of talk is that? If you're using that to claim the same thing about race mixing between whites and blacks, I ain't standing here no longer and listening to that goddam kind of talk. You won't see me standing still for that. I sure as hell wouldn't be Jim Whittaker if I did."

Jim turned and walked away without another word.

THREE

The argument between Grover and Jim Whittaker concerning Jeff Bazemore, which had ended so abruptly when Jim walked away in anger, had taken place almost thirteen years after a memorable Sunday afternoon shortly before Grover's twenty-fourth birthday.

It had been the last Sunday of September then in that brief season of the year when late summer could quickly become early autumn. It had always been a time of year between the seasons when the weather at the edge of the plateau was so changeable that one night there might be a killing frost and the next day a clear blue sky would suddenly become darkened from horizon to horizon by a threatening thunderhead.

The day in that long-ago year had been warm and sunny at the stables when Grover saddled Governor, his spirited big bay Tennessee walking horse, and rode off with a hammer and a pouch of ten- and twenty-penny nails to inspect the outside fencing for loose boardings. The weekly horseback ride around the farm had come to be an enjoyable Sunday chore since it was the one time in the week when he could ride for several hours and let Governor have a free rein to gallop as much as he pleased.

As usual on Sundays for the past two years since giving up his studies in business administration at the university and coming home to manage the Danford pony farm following the death of both parents in an automobile accident, Grover had been alone at the stables since early that morning. That was when Jim Whittaker, grumbling about it as he always did, had left to take his wife to her church in Wolverton. The stable boys and the two truck and tractor drivers, as they did every Sunday, were either at home or at a friend's house in Wolverton drinking beer and playing poker and nobody would be coming back to the stables until late afternoon at feeding and watering time.

After nearly an hour of riding, and finding very little

fence-fixing to do, Grover was at the southern boundary of the farm not far from the pond and weather shelter when he felt the first few drops of rain on his face. Governor felt the rain on his face, too, and he switched his tail several times and headed straight for the weather shelter.

The sky was only faintly gray when it began to rain, but the clouds quickly darkened as they came over the highland rim and the rain was soon falling in a steady drizzle. Within a few moments, the first streak of lightning could be seen against the low dark cloud, and strong gusts of wind began sweeping across the pasture. It was not long then until there was another zigzagging streak of lightning, and another and another in rapid succession, and then the thunder came crashing over the foothills. Almost at once the drizzle had turned into a drenching shower.

When the heavy rain began falling, Grover was only a hundred yards from the weather shelter, but by the time he could get to it, his shirt was soaking wet. After putting Governor in a stall, he took off his shirt and hung it on a bridle peg to dry as much as it would while he was waiting for the rain to stop.

All of the colts in the lower pasture, like excited children dashing for home when frightened by thunder and lightning, had galloped through the rain to the shelter. Crowded together and shoving one another, they were pawing and shaking their wet manes and switching their long tails as if impatient for the rain to stop so they could go back to where they had been grazing in the pasture.

After breaking open one of the bales of hay for the colts and putting some of it in the rack of Governor's stall, Grover was standing under the eaves of the shelter and watching the rain fall in a steady downpour when he saw a young woman running along the path between the fence and the railroad tracks. The path was only about fifty yards away, but she was going toward Wolverton, which was all of a mile distant, and there was not a single house nearby where she could go to wait for the rain to stop.

At first he hesitated to call to her to tell her to come to the weather shelter, because he knew she was already drenched by the rain. But as he watched her interestedly, he began to wonder who she was and why she had gone walking alone on Sunday afternoon. Even though she was not close enough for him to be able to see her face distinctly, he could see the youthful movement of her legs

29

and the agile motion of her slender hips as she ran, and he was more interested than ever.

Waiting no longer then, Grover called to her and waved his hand, beckoning her to hurry to the shelter. The girl stopped, standing there in the pouring rain in her clinging wet dress as though undecided about what to do, and Grover called her again and began waving urgingly with both arms.

"Hello, there!" he called more loudly than he had the first time. "Hurry up and come here out of that rain! Don't stay out there and keep on getting wet! Come in here!"

Still undecided, she glanced down the long path toward Wolverton. Then she wiped the rain from her face and eyes and looked at Grover again.

"Come on!" he urged her with a waving of his hand. "There's no gate—you'll have to climb over the fence! Hurry up! I don't want you to stay out there any longer!"

As if eager to please him then, the girl immediately ran to the fence, lifting her skirt as she went, and then, in order to climb over the high board fencing she pulled up her skirt until he could see the flashing contrast of some brief white underclothing against the pale brownness of her legs and thighs.

It was then, as she leaped from the fence and came running to Grover at the shelter, when he realized he had never before seen a white girl with such unusual coloring as hers. And as she came closer and he saw the brownish glow of her rainwet hair, he knew he had never before seen a mulatto or quadroon girl with her particular coloring.

Panting for breath, her large brown eyes wide with excitement, she stood there looking up at Grover and smiling cautiously with her dripping-wet yellow dress clinging to the bold contours of her breasts and hips.

While he was looking at her, wondering who she was and how she came to have such unusual coloring, her lips began to tremble as if she had suddenly become fearful of how she would be treated by a white man. She stepped backward and at the same time hurriedly glanced from side to side as if she might try to run away from him.

At that moment, and before a word had been spoken, lightning struck a tall oak tree close to the shelter, shattering the top limbs and splitting the trunk halfway to the ground. The deafening crash jarred the wooden building and frightened the colts so much that they reared, some of them standing on their hind legs, and whinnied nervously.

As if disdainful of the behavior of the colts, Governor snorted loudly and kicked his stall door.

Frightened by the closeness of the lightning bolt, just as the colts had been, the girl had reached out and was desperately clutching Grover's arm with both hands. Her whole body was trembling and she was whimpering like a frightened small child when Grover put his arms around her and held her close to him. With each breath she took, he could feel through the wetness of her dress the whole fullness of her breasts moving excitedly against his bare chest.

"I'm afraid—so afraid!" she said in a quavering cry.

"There's nothing to be afraid of now," he told her, patting her comfortingly. "This weather shelter is the safest place we could be. It's even got a lightning rod on the roof to take care of things for us."

"I can't help it—I'm always afraid," she said with the same sobbing quaver of her voice. "It always sounds so close—so loud—so terrifying—"

"You've been like this all your life?"

"Yes."

"Well, you won't have to be afraid anymore. The lightning will strike somewhere else next time. That's what I'll tell it to do. Now let me take care of all the worrying about it for you."

There was a quick tightening of the tension of her body for only an instant, almost like a grateful shudder, and after that she quickly pressed her face against him with a faintly murmured sigh.

"What's your name?" he asked her presently. "Who are you?"

Grover waited, and when she still did not tell him, he moved her away to arm's length so he could see her face. Looking at her then like that, he saw again the appealing warmth of her eyes and the pale brown tint of her skin and the sinuous bulge of her breasts under the wet yellow dress. He had been staring at her intently for such a long time, without a word said, that she began trembling again. Grover tightened his grip on her shoulders.

"I want to know who you are," he said impatiently, shaking her gently but firmly. "I've never seen you before. And I thought I knew everybody around here. What is your name?"

"Kathlee," she told him hesitantly.

"Kathlee?"

"Yes."

"Not Kathleen?"

"No. Kathlee."

"Where do you live?"

"Wolverton."

"How long?"

"About three weeks."

"That's why I've never seen you before. Where did you come to Wolverton from?"

"Memphis."

She glanced at him, expecting him to ask her why she would move from a city the size of Memphis to such a small country town. However, instead of asking her about it, he was staring at her intently.

"Kathlee," he then repeated with a slow nodding of his head. "Kathlee. That's a pretty name—pretty as you are. I've never known anybody with that name. I've never even heard it before. Maybe you're the only one who's ever had that name. But you're soaking wet, Kathlee!"

Gently shaking her shoulders again, he spoke to her with pretended sternness.

"You'll never get dry like this—you've got to do something about it."

"What do you want me to do?" she asked.

"Go behind those bales of hay and take off your wet clothes and wring out as much water as you can. Then hang them up to dry like I did my shirt. If you stay like this, you'll catch a bad cold, Kathlee."

She smiled then for the first time and, with girlish eagerness, turned to do as she had been told.

"But my dress is so wet. Do you want me to stay till my clothes are all dry again?"

"Of course, Kathlee," he told her. "Where would you be going without them?"

II

With the wet yellow dress clinging to the grown-up fullness of her body, Kathlee was giggling like a carefree young girl as she glanced backward over her shoulder just before going out of sight behind the bales of hay.

"I'm sorry there's no towel for you to use," he called to her.

"That's all right," he heard her say. "I won't need anything like that."

Grover was saying something to himself, almost talking out loud, when he walked away and stood under the dripping eaves of the shelter. He could see that it was still raining, lightly but steadily, and that a dark thunderhead was hovering like a huge black tent over the highland rim a few miles away with the threat of more lightning to come.

At any other time he knew he would have been standing there waiting impatiently for the rain to stop and worrying about all the rest of the fencing that needed to be inspected. Now, though, neither the rain nor the fencing could keep him from thinking about Kathlee and saying to himself that he had never known anyone like her before in his life. Kathlee and the pale brownness of her body. Kathlee and the eagerness of her smile. Kathlee and the softness of her touch. Kathlee and the goodness of her presence. Kathlee—Kathlee—Kathlee!

As he stood there staring blankly at the rain-soaked pasture he could see her so clearly again as she was climbing the high board fence and then running to him at the weather shelter in the rain, and then he was remembering how he had held her in his arms when the thunder frightened her and seeing again the gentle sway of her rounded slender hips as she went to take off her wet clothes. By then he knew that what he wanted was to be close to her again and to feel once more the warm softness of her face pressing against his chest.

Walking back and forth under the eaves, he found himself wondering what people would say if they found out that he had been with a colored girl in the weather shelter. But he quickly put that out of mind—to him now, white or colored, she was Kathlee.

Soon, though, there was the persistent thought about what would happen if he could not keep from being in love with a colored girl. Until then he would have sworn that nothing like that could happen to him. But now he was not so sure. He had never touched a colored girl before—not even when he was much younger and roaming the town one night with a crowd of boys who chased a Negro girl to the feed mill and bagging plant where several of them raped her in a freight car and left her crying. But Kathlee was different, he told himself over and over again, and not like any other woman white or colored. She was Kathlee and he wanted her no matter what happened.

When Grover left the dripping eaves and went back into the shelter, he saw that the colts were still stomping impatiently while waiting for the rain to stop. He broke open another bale of hay for them and pitched it into the feed racks. His big bay saddle horse, looking over the side of the stall and seeing the colts get another feeding, snorted and began kicking the stall boards as if to attract attention. Grover took some of the hay then and pitched it into Governor's rack and he was quiet again. Except for an occasional stomp of a hoof, the colts were quietly eating at the hay racks and the only sound of the rain was the faint splashing of water dripping from the roof to the puddles under the eaves.

Going to a bench, Grover sat down to wait while Kathlee was drying her clothes behind the tall stack of baled hay. As he sat there staring at the stack, once more he began thinking about her from the time she climbed over the fence until she went out of sight behind the bales. The longer he sat there thinking about her, the more anxious he became to see her and be close to her again.

When he could wait no longer, he called to her.

"Kathlee! Are your clothes almost dry now?"

"No," she answered at once as if she had been anxiously waiting for him to speak to her. "It's this damp weather."

"But aren't they almost dry enough to wear?"

"Not quite yet."

"How soon?"

"Maybe in a little while."

Disappointed, he slumped down dejectedly on the bench. It was becoming late in the afternoon and the dark thunderhead was sinking lower over the highland rim and turning the day into twilight. A sudden gust of wind swept through the shelter and a moment later a heavy shower of rain began beating on the roof.

"Kathlee, do you hear that," he called to her. "It's more rain coming down. You can't leave here and go home when it's raining like this. Your clothes would get soaking wet all over again."

"I don't mind how much it rains now just so there's no more thunder and lightning—and—and—if you'd tell me something—"

"What do you want to know?"

"Your name—that is—if you want to tell me." She spoke with a cautious hesitancy. "But if you don't want to—"

"Of course I'll tell you," he said, laughing a little. "It's no secret. I forgot all about it—I guess I was thinking about something more important all this time. About somebody named Kathlee. But my name is Grover—Grover Danford. And this is my place. This farm."

"And all those pretty ponies, too?"

"Yes. Ponies and everything."

34

"I always wanted a pony when I was little. A pony of my own I could ride and ride and ride."

"I'm afraid it's too late now for you to do that. You're a big girl now. But if you were about nine or ten years old—"

"I like to look at them, anyway. And I've seen that big white house up on the ridge. Is that where you and your family live?"

"It's where I live. I don't have a family—my parents are dead."

There was a long silence.

"But you're married, aren't you?" she asked then.

"No. I'm not married. Are you?"

"No."

The patter of rain on the roof was becoming louder.

"Kathlee, will you tell me more about you—about yourself?" he called to her.

"Yes! Oh, yes!" she said without hesitation.

"And will you come back here again?"

Several moments passed before she spoke.

"I don't know—I don't know if I should—because I'm not like—"

"Not like some other people? Is that what you mean?"

"Yes."

"If I tell you that makes no difference to me, will you believe me—and come back again?"

"Of course—if you want me to."

"You promise?"

"I promise."

"Even if it's thundering and lightning?"

"I'd run even faster then to get here."

"And if it's raining hard and your clothes get all soaking wet again?"

"I won't mind. I can always take them off and wring them out."

"But it takes so long for them to get dry. And I have to sit here and wait all this time."

Suddenly, with a startling brilliance in the darkened afternoon, a bolt of lightning zigzagged from the thunderhead over the highland rim. Then almost at the same instant so loud was the crash of thunder that it sounded as if the lightning had struck the weather shelter. The frightened colts reared and whinnied, and this time, regardless of the rain, they dashed out of the shelter in a noisy stampede.

III

As the colts were leaving, Governor was pounding the stall boarding with his hind hoofs and, as though she had held her breath as long as possible, Kathlee screamed with a cry of fright.

Before Grover could call to her and try to keep her from being afraid, Kathlee ran to him at the bench and locked her arms around his neck with a desperate grip. He could feel the frightened beating of her heart as she clung to him and sobbed with fear, and he quickly put his arms around her and patted her soothingly.

"It's all right now, Kathlee. It's all right."

"I can't help it," she sobbed. "I'm so afraid."

"It's all over now, Kathlee," he whispered. "That was the last one. There won't be any more lightning. No more thunder. Nothing more to be afraid of."

"How do you know?"

"The sky is clearing. It's already getting lighter."

"Are you sure?"

"Yes, Kathlee. Open your eyes and you'll see."

With her face pressed tightly against him, he could feel her shaking her head as if still afraid to open her eyes. He tightened his arms around her and instantly she snuggled closer as though wanting him to keep on holding her in his arms like that and never let her go.

"Does a storm always scare you like this?" he asked.

"I can't help it," she answered with a quick tightening of her arms around his neck. "I just can't help it. I've always been afraid of thunder and lightning ever since I was a little girl. Whenever there was a storm like that, my mother always held me on her lap and hugged me till all the thunder and lightning went away. And if the storm came in the middle of the night, she'd get in bed with me and hold me tight till morning. She always told me that as long as I was a good girl the thunder and lightning would never hurt me."

"Where was that?"

"We lived in Tupelo."

"Is that where you were born?"

"Yes."

"Do your parents still live there?"

"My mother does. I don't know about my father. I mean—my real father. I don't know where he lives. I never saw him."

"Why not?"

"He was a white man."

36

"How do you know he was a white man?"

"My mother told me."

"What else did she tell you about him?"

"I don't remember anything else now."

"Did he live in Tupelo?"

"I don't know. But I suppose so."

"Have you ever been curious about him? Have you ever wished you could see him—see what he looks like?"

"Of course. Many times. I still wish I could. But I don't ever expect to see him or recognize him if I did. That's too improbable—there're so many white men—"

"How long ago was it when your mother told you about your father?"

"It seems like a long time ago. I'm twenty-two years old now."

"Did you come here from Tupelo?"

"No. I came here from Memphis. I went to college in Memphis. I was there four years. I had a part-time job in a hospital and my mother sent me a little money and I graduated not long ago. I'm sure I was my mother's favorite and that's why she worked so hard to send me a little money so I could stay in college and graduate. I had seven brothers and sisters—they were half brothers and sisters—and they were a lot darker, really black, and they said my color was too light to make me kin to them. My mother tried to make them stop saying that but they never would. They teased me about my light color and straight hair so much that my mother said she wanted me to go away from home as soon as I finished high school and get the best college education I could."

She paused as if trying to decide if she would say anything more about herself.

"Kathlee," Grover said then, "did your other father, the one you lived with, help you get through college?"

"No!" she said emphatically. "That father—I don't mean my real father, I mean the other one—he beat me a lot of times because he said I wasn't black like him and my brothers and sisters. I was in my last year of high school then and sometimes he would get up in the middle of the night and beat me in bed with his fists and then throw me on the floor and kick me, and my mother cried but couldn't make him stop hurting me. It was awful. He hurt me so much. But I stayed so I'd have my high school diploma and could get into college."

Nothing was said after that for a long time. The rain had stopped and the clouds were drifting away and the sun was setting in a fiery glow behind the barns and stables. Presently, in the quiet of the twilight, Grover tightened his arms around Kathlee and moved her to his lap and held her closer to him. He wanted to know more about her early life in Tupelo but, after her telling him about having been beaten so much, he decided it would be better to wait until some other time.

"Kathlee, you still must be a good girl like your mother told you to be," he said lightly, "because that storm didn't hurt you this time. Are you, Kathlee?"

She nodded quickly. "I am—I am."

"Even when you're like this—with no clothes on?"

Looking up at him with a shy glance, she laughed in her girlish manner.

"You told me to take them off."

"Do you always do everything somebody tells you to do?"

Catching her breath, she hesitated for several moments.

"No," she said then with emphatic firmness. "Only what you want me to do."

"Do you really mean that?"

"Yes."

"Anything?"

"Anything."

"Then stay like you are now, Kathlee," he told her in an exaggerated manner of command. "Your clothes won't be dry enough for you to wear for a long time. I'll tell you when you can put them on. You hear, Kathlee?"

"I hear," she whispered, pressing her face against him.

He shook her gently.

"Look here! Have you forgotten my name already?"

"No! Grover—Grover—Grover!"

"Then don't ever forget from now on, Kathlee."

"I won't—Grover—I won't! Never—never!"

FOUR

It was long after five o'clock in the slightly hazy afternoon. Kathlee had promised to meet him at the weather shelter at four o'clock that Sunday afternoon for the second time, and Grover, anxiously watching the path between the white-painted fence and the railroad tracks, wished he had asked her to meet him days sooner and had not waited a whole week before seeing her again.

Grover had already gone to the fence and back several times, and each time when he had failed to see Kathlee coming up the path from Wolverton he had become increasingly worried about what might have happened to her.

Unlike the previous Sunday afternoon with thunder and lightning and downpour of rain, the day had been clear and bright with only a few small flecks of white clouds high in the sky until the coming of the smoky haze.

Since it was not raining and there was no threat of a thunderstorm, the only reason Grover could think of for Kathlee not being at the weather shelter at the time they had agreed upon was that she had been followed up the path when she left Wolverton to meet him. And if she had been followed, he kept on thinking over and over again, somebody could have caught up with her and taken her out of sight into the tall bushes that grew close to the railroad tracks.

What had made him so disturbed and was keeping him worried was recalling so clearly what Jim Whittaker had said early in the past week.

They were at the stables that Tuesday morning when Jim told Grover about having heard a lot of talk on the street and in some of the stores in Wolverton about a light-skinned, brown-haired colored girl about twenty-two or twenty-three years old who was the new teacher at the Negro public school that year and was so good-looking that it was said to be a sure bet that it would not be long until some white man caught up with her. Jim said he had not actually seen the colored girl himself, but that so much had been said about her that he was willing to believe she was at least half as good-looking from head to toe and all between as some of the men had described her as being. As Jim commented then, that would be enough to send a whole crowd of men hurrying out to see what they could do about their femaling notions.

"You listen to some of that kind of talk and before you know it you can feel those notions creeping into you under your own skin," Jim had told Grover. "That's a natural thing to happen to a man. But I try to be a good family man to my old woman at my age and as a rule I stay pretty goddam close to home these days. You'll see me taking my old woman to her church preaching on Sunday mornings and you won't find me downtown on Saturday nights getting drunk and raising hell in general no more. That's all in the past—drunk and hell-raising. And that's what happens to you when you get to be a settled married man like me.

"Just the same, and I ain't ashamed to admit it, and I could boast about it if you pushed me, I've done my share of colored-girl femaling in my time and that's why I couldn't let myself judge against any white man who wants to and can these days. Of course, what I'm talking about is when you do that kind of colored femaling on the side. Not the kind of race mixing when a black and a white come right out in the open and live under the same roof or even try to get married—that's where I draw the line and a goddam ten-foot line at that. But putting aside that kind of out-and-out race mixing, times don't change otherwise enough so you'd notice it and just as long as there are some good-looking high yellow girls to be sighted, they're going to get chased and caught in a hurry by some white men. Of course, some of those high yellows are going to run faster than others—or a hell of a lot slower, if you want to look at it that way.

"You notice how I get all worked up when I start talking like this, boy? Well, maybe it's because I've been around a long time and seen a lot more than young people like you know about. You'd think the new generation in Wolver County would act different in these days and times and not keep up the old standard ordinary way of femaling. I hate to see that kept up in these modern times because I don't think it's right and always did feel sorry for a young colored girl who got sighted by a white man and don't nearly ever have a fair chance to pick and choose for herself. What the hell! The only fair thing to do is let her have as much say-so as a white man. That might start a

40

loud argument about it all over the place and draw a big crowd, but if they went about it fair and square by flipping heads or tails, or something like that, she'd at least have a fifty-fifty chance of having her own way. But like it is around here now, I don't look for that high yellow schoolteacher to get a chance to flip a dime or quarter and call heads or tails. I know too many people around Wolverton who'd say to hell with that and go about it the usual way.

"Now, Grover, if it's pretty much true what I heard said about that schoolteacher, it's a goddam shame she ain't a white woman and all that good-looking instead of being a high yellow—"

Jim paused for a moment and looked at Grover with a meaningful nodding of his head.

"Well, boy, I'm going to come right out and say it. If she was the other, I wouldn't let up one goddam minute trying to get you to go about it yourself before somebody else did. Why? Because I'm worried about you, boy, that's why. I've known you since the day you got born and you're just like a favorite son to me. You own this fine pony farm your daddy left you free and clear and you're making real good money all the time and don't have a worry in the world. But you're not getting any younger and you're still fooling around and wasting your time and living in that big house up there all by yourself and not getting married like you ought to be by now. I know you go off to see women in Nashville and Memphis pretty often. That's all right because it shows your mind runs in the right direction. But you don't never come back here married. That's what's wrong. Now, let me tell you something, boy. If you wait too long, the time's coming when you'll wake up in the middle of the night feeling goddam desperate for a woman in the bed with you and that's when you'll jerk on your goddam pants and rush out and marry the exact wrong woman to be good for you. I'd hate to see that happen to you, boy. It'd be a goddam shame."

After listening all that time to Jim Whittaker, Grover had walked away without saying anything, but Jim, still talking, had followed him out of the stable.

"Grover, when a man wakes up in the middle of the night sweating enough hot lather to shave with and rushes off without stopping long enough to piss and marries the wrong woman, he's begging for as much goddam misery as a young girl is going to get if she's thrown down and raped by some goddam stinking bastard who wouldn't even wait around long enough afterward to help her look for

41

her drawers to put back on. The only difference is that a man ought to have better sense and a young girl can't always help herself. You've got enough sense to outsmart that kind of misery for yourself. Now go ahead and use it."

As Grover walked away from Jim then, it had been the beginning of his being disturbed and worried by the fear that somebody might follow Kathlee up the path from Wolverton and rape her before she could get to the weather shelter the next time they were to meet.

II

By the end of the week, after worrying day after day, Grover still had not been able to think of a way to meet Kathlee so she would not have to walk a mile both coming and going along the lonely path.

When he and Kathlee had talked about it the previous Sunday, both of them realized that if he came for her in his car, and anybody saw her riding through town with him, it would be reported to the school superintendent and she would not be allowed to teach another day in Wolverton and would have to go back to Memphis. And even if he went for her after midnight and took her to his house, they knew there would still be the risk of somebody seeing a colored girl get into a white man's car and go away with him.

When Grover looked at his watch again, another half hour had passed and in a few minutes it would be six o'clock. And now that it would soon be two hours after the time that Kathlee had said she would come to the weather shelter, he wondered if she had changed her mind about seeing him again and had not even left home to meet him.

As he walked restlessly back and forth under the shelter, he took the small jewelry box out of his pocket and gazed at it sadly. He remembered how eager and happy he had been when he was selecting a present for Kathlee and now he wondered if he would ever be able to give it to her.

He was still looking at the golden wrapping around the present when he heard somebody calling him. He was sure he recognized Kathlee's voice when she called more urgently the second time and he put the box back into his pocket and ran from the shelter. Kathlee was standing on the outside of the high board fence and she waved to him as soon as she saw him. This time she was wearing a dress in a much lighter shade of yellow, but as she climbed over the high fencing, he could see the familiar flashing contrast of her brief white underclothing against the pale brownness of her legs.

Kathlee ran straight to him then and locked her arms around him as tightly as she could, like a frightened child wanting to be with somebody she could trust to protect her. As she clung to him, she was panting for breath as if she had been running all the way from Wolverton. Grateful to have her in his arms again, Grover held her close to him and waited for her to get her breath back. Her face and arms were warm and damp.

"Grover—I'm sorry," she said presently, speaking slowly as her breath came back to her. "I'm so sorry—I didn't want to be late like this. I wanted to be here with you all the time—just as I promised—but I couldn't help it, Grover."

"What was the matter?" he asked in a tense quickness of voice, unable to think of any reason for her being so late other than that she had been followed. "What happened? Did somebody stop you—bother you—anything—when you were coming up the path?"

"No," she answered at once. "No. Nothing like that. I ran all the way from town as fast as I could and didn't see anybody."

"Then what did happen?"

He could feel her body tremble as she pressed her face, still warm and damp, tightly against him. Picking her up, he carried her into the shelter and sat down on the bench with her on his lap.

"I want you to tell me about it, Kathlee," he said gravely. He felt relieved knowing that nobody had followed her up the path from town, but he was still worried about what else could have happened that had kept her from meeting him for more than two hours. He was trying to keep from thinking about it, but everything that Jim Whittaker had said kept coming back to his mind. "Kathlee, I want to know all about it. Everything. The truth. Now tell me."

"I'll have to tell you about it from the beginning."

"All right. Tell me from the beginning."

"You'll believe me, won't you?"

"I will if you say I can."

"Please do—you must."

"Then what is it?"

"There was this man—"

"Who was it? What's his name?"

He knew immediately that he was hurt and angry and he knew how rough and demanding his voice sounded when he spoke. And that was when he realized for the first time that he was completely in love with her and jealous and never wanted her to be with any other man.

"What man?" he said again in an even harsher manner.

"Please don't stop loving me!" she begged.

"How do you know I love you?"

"Because I love you!"

"You really do?"

"Yes, Grover! And you've got to love me—you must! Please say you love me! I want you to so much!"

She looked up at him momentarily, as if silently pleading with him to be kind and understanding and not to stop loving her. Faintly sobbing, she then quickly lowered her head with a tightening of her arms around him. He had never been in love before and, no matter what had happened that she still had not told him about, he did not want to wait any longer to assure her that he did love her.

"How did you find out that I love you, Kathlee?"

"I don't know exactly—it's just that I love you so much and I want you to love me too."

"Even since last Sunday when it took so long for your clothes to get dry? Was that when it was, Kathlee?" He felt a brief trembling of her body.

"I think so. Yes. I'm sure about it now. It was last Sunday, Grover."

"I do love you, Kathlee. I'll always love you."

"Don't ever stop, Grover. Please don't ever stop."

He put his hand under her chin and raised her head until he could look into her eyes.

"There's nobody else, is there, Kathlee?"

She quickly shook her head. "No, Grover. Nobody."

"Is that the truth? Can I believe you?"

"It is the truth. Please believe me."

"Then what about this man you were talking about? And why were you so late getting here?"

"I want to tell you everything, Grover. Everything. And you must believe me. You've got to!"

"Then what is it?"

"In Memphis—there was this man—while I was in college—"

"What about him? What did he want?"

"He wanted me to marry him and—"

"A white man?"

"No."

"Then he was colored—a Negro—"

"Yes. Black."

"Is that all?"

"I wish it had been. But that was only the beginning. It was almost a year ago now. My last year in college. His name is Willy Shoelong. He's a barber in Memphis. That's what he claims to be, but he's not really a barber—he's something else—he's horrible!"

"Tell me what happened."

"He saw me on the street the first time and wanted a date. But I didn't like the way he looked and the way he talked and I didn't want to have anything to do with him. But that didn't stop him. He followed me several times to try to find out where I lived and I was so afraid of him that until he'd gone away I'd go to the college library or visit a girl I knew and never went straight home to where I roomed with another girl. I was afraid of him—there was something about the way he looked and talked that made me feel so uneasy. I was always thinking he might kill me. He was tall and thin with large round eyes that looked as if they would pop out of his head any minute and he carried a knife that he'd take out of his pocket and open the blade while he was talking.

"And whenever he could stop me on the street, and right up to the time I graduated, he'd tell me that if I didn't marry him nobody else would and live to know it. I always told him that I was going to be a schoolteacher and wasn't thinking of getting married. That didn't stop him from talking about what he'd do, though, and he said he'd find out wherever I went to teach and keep after me till I did what he wanted. That's why I came to Wolverton —I didn't think he'd ever find me here. It's such a small town and I didn't tell anybody where I was going to teach —but somehow he found out where I am."

III

Grover wanted to believe she was being truthful and would not try to deceive him, but he was not certain and could not keep from being hurt and resentful. It was the first time that there had been any suspicion in his mind and he could not keep from thinking that she had been unfaithful that afternoon while he was waiting for her at the weather shelter.

"Was he here today, Kathlee?" he demanded with a rough rising of his voice.

"Yes."

"Then you've been with him!"

"No—not exactly," she protested earnestly. "No. Not

45

like that—not the way you mean. That's the truth, Grover. You've got to believe me."

At once, without another word, Grover moved her away from his lap to the bench and left her sitting there as he walked across the shelter to the stall where Governor was contentedly eating hay and occasionally switching his tail and stomping a hoof. Leaning over the top board of the stall, he slapped Governor's rump several times with affectionate pats and then he stood there for a long time wanting the company of his horse and not wanting to face Kathlee while his mind was racing with suspicion about what might have taken place that afternoon between her and the Negro barber from Memphis.

For a whole week he had been thinking of her as he wanted her to be—Kathlee, neither white nor colored, only Kathlee—and not once had it come to mind that a Negro man would try to make love to her as he had done only a week before. His only worry since then was that she would be raped by a white man and now he was even more upset and worried knowing that a Negro man wanted her and he knew he had to find out for his own peace of mind what had actually happened that afternoon. With every thought that flashed through his mind being a piercing pain, he turned around with a nervous twisting of his body and looked straight at Kathlee.

She had not moved from the bench and she was sitting there watching him with a tense clasping of her hands on her lap. Her eyes and lips and the whole expression of her face pleaded with him not to keep on staring at her in such an accusing manner. Her mouth twitched with a nervous smile.

"What did you mean by what you said just now—not exactly?" he demanded, his voice rough and loud. "Not exactly! What does that mean?"

"There was nothing like the way we did last Sunday, Grover. That's what I'm trying to tell you. Nothing at all."

"And you didn't undress for him?"

Shaking her head, she tried to smile reassuringly.

"No, Grover." She spoke as calmly as she could. "I was in the house all the time, Grover, and the Lawsons made him stay on the front porch and wouldn't let him come inside. They locked all the doors and windows and told him if he tried to break in they'd call the police and have him arrested. He kept on saying all he wanted to do was talk to me for a little while and wouldn't make any trouble for anybody if they'd let him in the house. I told the Lawsons I was afraid he'd hurt me, because I knew he

46

would if I didn't promise to do what he wanted, and they were so afraid of him by that time that they told him again to go away or they'd call the police and have him put in jail. Finally, he said if the Lawsons promised not to tell the police he was in Wolverton that he'd promise to leave and go back to Memphis. Grover, that's exactly what happened and that's why I couldn't leave to get here sooner."

Grover had come closer to Kathlee and he stood there looking down at her as if trying to convince himself that she had been truthful and would not deceive him about what had happened.

"Well, if you say he didn't go into the house where you were—"

"No, Grover, he didn't."

"Where is he now?"

"He went back to Memphis."

"How do you know he did?"

"I'm sure he was so afraid then that the Lawsons were going to call the police anyway, that that's why he left in a hurry. He ran out to his car and drove off as fast as he could. Willy Shoelong has been arrested a lot of times in Memphis and his picture has been in the newspapers and he was afraid the Wolverton police would be real hard on him if they caught him here and found out who he really was."

Grover sat down on the bench beside her.

"Willy Shoelong. Is that his real name?"

"That's the way it is in the newspapers every time he's arrested."

"What did he say to you all that time while he was at Pete Lawson's house?"

"Mostly the same things he'd said before in Memphis. Trying to get me to marry him—so he could make me go out with other men and get money to give him. I know that's the real reason he tries to get me to marry him for. And this time there was something else he'd never said before. When he left the Lawson house—he said—" Kathlee closed her lips tightly.

"What did he say?"

"He said—he'd kill me if I ever lived with anybody else except him—or did anything like that—married or not."

"That's already happened, Kathlee."

"I know it has."

Nothing was said after that for a long time while he sat there thinking about what Kathlee had told him. All doubt and suspicion had vanished from his mind and he knew he could believe her completely after that. Now, however, he was concerned and worried about the threat Willy Shoelong had made.

"This is serious," he said presently. "I'm going to talk to my lawyer tomorrow and find out what he advises. I was seeing him about another matter, anyway, but first of all now I want to find out how to keep you from being threatened like that anymore. Something's got to be done about it."

Once again he was silent while he gazed at his horse in the stall on the other side of the weather shelter. He could not keep from worrying, now that Willy Shoelong knew where Kathlee was living, about the constant danger of his coming back to Wolverton.

She touched his arm with her hand. "Grover—"

He turned and looked at her.

"Grover, don't worry so much about me now. We're here and nothing else matters while we're together like this. It might be another whole week again—"

"No, it won't," he told her emphatically. "It's not going to be that long again. I'm not going to wait another week to see you. That's too much of a waste of time. And suppose I thought of something I wanted to tell you before then, or had something to give you—"

Reminded then of what he had already brought to give her, he reached into his pocket for the jewelry box and handed it to her.

"But in the meantime I already have something for you, Kathlee. If you'll try it on right away, we'll see if it fits—and if you like it."

She quickly unwrapped the narrow box, smiling excitedly, and saw the gold necklace sparkling with settings of small diamonds.

"Grover—" She had caught her breath as tears filled her eyes. "Grover—it's so beautiful—and you gave it to me. I'm so happy—Grover—I want to say something—but I don't know what to say now—"

"You don't have to say anything, Kathlee. I want to say something. I love you, Kathlee. And if you love me, that's all that matters."

"Oh, I do—I do!" She looked at him, her eyes blinking with tears, and then quickly locked her arms around his neck. "Oh, Grover! I love you so much! I do—I do! I know my color is different—but I can't help it—and I want to belong to you like I am. Always! I do—I do! Always!"

FIVE

Grover Danford, having slept only a few hours after midnight, had got up at dawn Monday morning and cooked his own breakfast and finished eating before Annie and Della came to work as usual at seven o'clock. It was still not yet eight o'clock when he left the house and walked down the path to the stables. When he got there, Jim Whittaker was just arriving to go to work for the day.

"What are you doing down here this early, Grover?" Jim said with suspicious gruffness. "Are you checking up on me to see if I'm being late getting to work? I don't want nobody snooping around here. I get my work done, and always have. Nobody has to hold a watch to time me. Besides, you'll be in my way if you don't go on off somewhere."

"It's nothing like that, Jim," Grover was quick to assure him. "It's got nothing to do with you. Think nothing of it, Jim. I was up early because I want to hurry downtown this morning to see Ben Dowd about something important."

"Well, if that's the true reason, then you could've stayed in bed and slept a couple hours more for all the good it'll do you. Ben Dowd is just like the rest of those lawyers. They don't show up at their offices before ten o'clock—unless they're trying a case in court and can see a goddam big fee they can pick out of somebody's pocket. But there'll be one case in police court this morning that I bet lawyers won't have a chance to get rich on. Being who got arrested, and what he done, I'll bet you a quarter out of my pocket right now that Judge Painter won't take more than a quick minute to give him the limit and sentence him to a year at hard labor—and all that before the lawyers can wash the sleep out of their eyes."

"Who are you talking about, Jim? Who got arrested?"

"You've read in the newspapers about Willy Shoelong—"

"Who? Who did you say?"

Grover knew he had distinctly heard the name, but he was so surprised that it was hard to believe that Jim could be talking about the same person who had threatened Kathlee.

"Willy Shoelong, that's who. He's that Negro barber in Memphis who's always in trouble with the law for selling dope and running women and such things. But he couldn't have the time to do much barbering if he's always doing so much oustide the law like they say about him in the papers. Seems like hardly a week goes by——"

"What about him, Jim?" Grover asked anxiously. "What did he do?"

"You didn't hear about it?"

"No. But he didn't try to kill somebody, did he, Jim?"

"In a way, yes. I'd say that. The police saw him speeding about sixty miles an hour going out Union Street late yesterday afternoon just before six o'clock and they chased him and forced his car in a ditch before he could get out of town. The way I heard it, when they got out to arrest him for speeding, he pulled a knife on them. That's when he might've killed somebody if they hadn't kicked the knife out of his hand and slugged him. Maybe Willy Shoelong can pull a knife on the police in Memphis and get away with it, but not in Wolverton he won't. The way the police run this town, and lawyer or no lawyer, he'll get a year at hard labor for that and not just a ten-dollar fine for speeding. The Wolverton police and Judge Painter make up their minds about that beforehand."

"Are you sure about all this, Jim?"

"I'm goddam sure. I heard it straight out of the police station. And it's Monday morning now, too. That makes a big difference. Toward the end of the week, like Thursday or Friday, the police court generally goes a little bit easier on people for being drunk on the street or wife beating and things like that and will even listen to lawyers talk. But not on Monday mornings they won't. The way I like to explain that is because everybody's been to church preaching on Sunday and got so much religion that it spills over to the next day. That's why they like to start the week being hard on sinning people who've been in shooting and knifing scrapes Saturday night, or ordinary fornicating, and that's when Judge Painter gives them the limit with no back talk allowed. That's the reason why you can count on them putting Willy Shoelong out of business for a whole solid year—barbering and all the rest."

"Well, that's a good thing to know about somebody like him," Grover remarked vaguely, so relieved that he could think of nothing else to say about it then. After gazing down the slope in the direction of Wolverton for several moments, he nodded to Jim and started walking toward the stable office. "Let's go inside and go over the books some, Jim. We haven't looked at the accounts for a while now and I've decided I don't have to rush downtown to see Ben Dowd right away. I'll give him a little more time to get the sleep washed out of his eyes—like you said about it."

"Goddam lawyers," Jim was saying as he went into the stable with Grover. "Sleep late in the morning and read forty words out of their lawbooks and slap a lien on a poor man's chattels if he can't hand over forty dollars in cash when they snap their fingers."

After spending nearly three hours in the stable office, Grover got into his car to drive to Wolverton.

II

It was only a little more than a mile from the cluster of barns and stables to Wolverton but since he was driving slowly as he thought about his reason for seeing his attorney, it was close to eleven o'clock when Grover got out of his car in the parking lot behind the Citizens Fidelity Bank. Ben Dowd's office was on the second floor above the bank and could be reached by a narrow wooden stairway on the outside of the two-story building.

When he got to the top floor and opened the office door, Ben's elderly secretary, Mrs. Houser, regarded him in her usual impersonal manner as though she had never seen him before in her life and considered him to be an intruder who had not been properly introduced. Ben always said that Mrs. Houser was the ideal secretary for him because she was the personification of law and order, professional integrity, strict morality, and saintly motherhood, whereas a younger and more personable secretary in his office would hardly alter his reputation of being more of a dedicated playboy and roguish bachelor than the competent attorney he really was.

Tight-lipped and stern-faced and dressed in her customary high-necked white blouse and prim-lengthed black skirt, her sparse gray hair drawn rigidly over her head to a bun on the back of her neck, Mrs. Houser made no sign of recognition and gave no greeting as she regarded Grover from her desk where she sat stiffly erect in her straight-back, cane-bottom chair that looked as if it had been brought to the office from her kitchen. In fact, it was an old-fashioned kitchen chair. She had told Ben to provide it for her because men had purposely designed modern office chairs in such a way that a secretary's lower limbs would be indecently exposed.

No matter who entered Ben Dowd's office, stranger or not, Mrs. Houser always gave the immediate impression that an endurance contest was in progress to decide whether she or the visitor would be the first to speak. Even though she had been the office secretary for only seven years, in appearance she had long before that reached the stage in life when age was no longer to be reckoned in years or even in decades but as a lifetime.

Ben Dowd, who was still not yet into his forties at the time, always took delight in observing the puzzled reactions of visiting politicians and businessmen when they were confronted by Mrs. Houser upon entering his office for the first time.

Usually the first thing a startled visitor said, after he was behind the closed door of Ben's inner office, was to express amazement that a young lawyer would have as his secretary the grandmotherly Mrs. Houser in her kitchen chair at the reception desk.

This was when Ben, his face beaming with an unsuppressible grin, would try to say with all seriousness that he had been waiting seven years for Mrs. Houser to make the first mistake in her typing or misplace a document in the files so he would have an excuse to fire her and get a pretty young secretary with visible bosom and legs.

In contrast, Ben Dowd had the appearance, and somewhat of a justified reputation, of being carefree and sportive in his personal life, although behind his jolly round-faced countenance was keen and astute legal ability. Financially successful, still unmarried, and comfortably stout for his six-foot height, he had never had the desire to be associated with a law partner or to attain any political office.

However, year after year, always obscure in the background and never seen in the forefront, Ben was the ruling force in county politics, and not to an inconsiderable extent in state politics, and his county political organization rarely failed to get a Democrat of his choice elected or appointed to office.

When asked why he had already waited so long to get married and give a worthy young woman a comfortable life with accompanying social status, Ben would say he was waiting for a drastic drop in the national divorce rate so he would get better odds for that kind of a gamble. In the meanwhile, however, he was keeping quite a few women —many of them being young divorcees and recent widows

—hopefully interested in him as a prospective husband and provider so that he would have a wide field to select from when he was ready to make such a commitment.

Finally, after a long interval of silence, the endurance contest between Mrs. Houser and Grover ended when Mrs. Houser, with an exasperated sigh of surrender, asked Grover what he wanted.

"I want to see Ben Dowd," he told her with a broad smile that she could only interpret as being a gloating show of victory over her.

He was on the verge of asking Mrs. Houser if she could think of any other reason for his being there when she spoke to him again in her curt manner.

"Mr. Danford, do you have an appointment with Mr. Dowd?"

He shook his head.

"Then I'll be glad to arrange an appointment for you. What day would—"

"Make it for right now, Mrs. Houser. This is when I want to see him—not tomorrow or the next day. I couldn't wait that long."

There was a tight closing of her lips as if she would never speak to him again. Before she could say anything then, he went to the door of the inner office, rapped on it loudly, and then opened it and went into Ben's office.

Ben, listening to somebody on the telephone, pointed to a chair in front of his desk as Grover was closing the door behind him. After listening for a while longer, Ben mumbled a few words before putting down the phone. It was an unusually large room with thick green carpeting and, in addition to the massive leather-topped desk and several high-back chairs, the principal furnishings were a dozen green-leather armchairs carefully spaced around a wide mahogany conference table. On the pale green walls were numerous large gilt-framed pictures of horses and ponies and placid scenes of streams and fields and woodland.

After putting down the phone, Ben reached over the desk and turned a large framed photograph around for Grover to see. It was a full-length photograph in color of a smiling blond-haired girl about twenty years old who was darkly suntanned and wearing a scanty two-piece bathing suit.

"Grover, I want to introduce you to a newfound friend of mine who lives over in Jackson," Ben said in a grave tone of voice as if actually making a formal introduction. Then with a grin he added, "You may call her Gladys.

53

But on one condition. I give my consent and permission subject to withdrawal if you don't stay on your side of the fence. Remember that. Anyhow, Gladys is crazy about the grandness of nature and the great outdoors. You can tell that about her by the way she looks in a bathing suit, can't you, bub?"

Grover nodded.

"Fine, fine!" Ben said with a glowing smile, leaning back in his chair and clasping his hands behind his head. "You own part of the great outdoors with that pony farm of yours and I thought you'd appreciate one of nature's landmarks. I'm glad you've got such good perception, bub. And while we're at it, there's one more thing I want to tell you about Gladys. And this concerns you."

"How does it concern me?"

"She's as crazy as can be about horseback riding. Now, if Gladys comes over from Jackson someday soon for an outing I want you to fix her up with a good saddle horse—not one of those little ponies, of course, for a fully developed young woman like her—so she can ride and ride to her heart's content over the hills and dales at your place. But don't be surprised if she wants to ride bareback instead of with saddle—she's the kind of girl to have a notion like that."

"Sure, Ben," Grover agreed immediately. "I'll let her ride Governor. He'll be a good horse for her. Governor can give a strange man a rough ride, but somehow he can tell the difference and likes to be nice and gentle with a woman."

"Fine, fine! I know Governor has got plenty of horse sense. I'll call Gladys on the phone and arrange for her to come over here soon for an outing. And before I forget it, there's still one more thing you ought to know in advance about Gladys just so you'll be well prepared and won't stand there staring at her slack-jawed like a damn fool and embarrass her."

"What do you mean, Ben?" Grover asked.

"I told you that she's crazy about the grandness of nature and the great outdoors and all that. But I'm not talking about walking in the rain and looking at sunsets and picnicking among the cow chips in a pasture. Well, the fact is, being a modern girl with free-thinking ideas and so on, she likes to combine sunbathing with horseback riding."

"Both at the same time?"

"That's right."

"How can she do that?"

"Just as I said," Ben told him. "She likes to ride a horse and get a suntan at the same time. See what I mean? But she wears riding boots and a jockstrap."

"A jockstrap! A girl—"

"I told you she's a modern free-thinking girl."

"I know, but a girl wearing only a jockstrap—"

"Don't forget the boots, bub."

Grover was shaking his head. "Ben, I'm talking about this other thing."

"If that bothers you, bub, what do you want to call it—an athletic supporter?"

Grover was still shaking his head. "But, Ben—at the stables—the stable boys—"

"That's nothing to worry about, bub," Ben told him with a wave of his hand. "Forget it. She'll probably have on a raincoat or something and won't take it off till she gets out of sight in the fields. But you don't have to follow her to find out, bub. Just take my word for it. And while I think about it, don't give her a whip and spurs when you saddle up Governor—I mean when you bridle him for her, because I'm afraid that might put some bad notions in her impressionable, free-thinking feminine mind. She might take a notion to mount me with a whip and spurs and give me a rough ride. I don't want her to get started doing that. Now! That's all settled. So what can I do for you, Grover? What did you want to see me about? Have you got a lawsuit in mind? Somebody owe you money for a pony you can't collect? What's troubling you?"

III

Grover was looking at the photograph on the desk and what he saw now was not blond-haired Gladys but a life-like picture of Kathlee smiling at him so lovingly the previous afternoon when she finally got to the weather shelter. That was when Ben suddenly reached over the desk and turned the photograph around until it faced him instead of Grover.

"No you don't, bub!" he said, shaking his head with a warning grimness. "That one is taken. You'll have to go somewhere and find your own."

"I already have, Ben," Grover stated seriously. "That's what I want to see you about."

"Who? What? Where? When?"

"Ben, she's the new teacher at the Negro school. Her name is Kathlee. She's a colored girl. And she's unusual. She has very pale brown skin and wavy brown hair—just like some white girls you've seen. Believe me, Ben, you can hardly tell the difference—"

"You're joking."

"I am not."

"A colored girl—a nigger girl—"

"Shut up!"

There was a long silence while he stared at Grover.

"All right," Ben said presently. "I'll take that back. I apologize. A colored girl. A girl of color. But what the hell, Grover?"

"I want to marry her."

"You said what?"

"You heard me. Marry her."

"Marry her! You damn fool! You Yankee! You foreigner! You Communist! What the hell!"

"I'm serious, Ben."

"You're out of your goddam mind—that's what! You're a white man. You can't do that. It'd be a Baptist sin. And it wouldn't be legal, anyhow. Mixed marriages are not permitted in this state. And if you went off to some other place and did it, I'd see to it that you got arrested if you ever set foot back here again. By God, I'd dig into the laws till I found the right one to hang you with. But right now what I'm thinking is to hurry and get you committed to the lunatic asylum. You'd be safe there till you could get nursed back into your right mind."

They sat there glaring at one another for a long time. Finally, with a grin spreading over his florid face, Ben Dowd was the first to speak.

"So you're the white man who got to her first. I've been hearing about her for the past couple of weeks—a lot of studs around here have had notions for her. But you got to her first, huh, bub? And what did you do, bub? Rape her and then get remorseful and think you ought to marry her? You're a real Southern gentleman, bub. I've got to admire you for that. I take off my hat to you. A real honest-to-god Southern gentleman is not easy to find these days. Most of them have gone up North or to Texas or some other godforsaken place. If I had a Confederate flag handy, I'd stand up and wave it at you. You son of a bitch!"

"Believe me, Ben, that's not the way it was."

"Well, whatever way it was, you can't marry her."

"Why not?"

"I've already told you it'd be an illegal marriage in the state. Rape or pregnancy or consent or nothing else would make any difference." His voice then was harsh and without a trace of sympathy. "It'd be illegal even if you could

56

get a marriage license—which you can't. No county clerk is going to risk going to jail for issuing a license for a mixed marriage. What the hell, Grover! That's some more reason enough, for God's sake. And even if the courts ever rule that interracial marriages are legal in the state, you'd be exiled—run out of the country by night riders, and there're plenty of them to do it, too. You'd never be able to live in this part of the world again. The Baptists and Methodists and Holy Rollers wouldn't stand for it. You'd have to give up that fine pony farm—everything you've got. You ought to stop and think how hard your daddy worked to build it up and leave you what you've got. Now, don't be a damn fool, Grover. Wake up!"

"But, Ben, I've never known anybody like her before— I can't give her up."

After a long, thoughtful pause, Ben smiled with a slow nodding of his head.

"All right. I believe you really mean it. And you don't have to give her up, bub. If you think you've got to have this colored girl like you say you do, I'll tell you how to go about it. There's a sensible way—a traditional way—the time-honored custom of mankind."

"What is it?"

"Keep her—keep her like a mistress—a concubine—or whatever you want to call it. You know what I mean. You'll have everything you want and nothing to lose—as long as you're not seen in public with her. You won't be the first one around Wolverton who worked things out that way. I've even known Baptists and Methodists to do the same thing on the side. And if those holy people do it, there's no reason why a Presbyterian—"

"That's not what I had in mind," Grover was quick to protest. "When I came in here to see you—"

"It's time for a recess," Ben told him abruptly, getting up and walking toward the door. "I've got a cramp in my leg and you've got a cramp in your brain. Let's go over to the club for a drink—and it might even take two or three drinks for what ails us."

As they were going through the outer office, Mrs. Houser got up from her chair to speak to Ben.

"Mr. Dowd, if there are some important phone calls for you, where can you be reached?"

"I don't want to be reached, Mrs. Houser."

"All right, Mr. Dowd," she said in her calmly efficient manner. "I won't call you at the club unless it's absolutely necessary."

On the way down the narrow wooden stairway to the

street, Ben said it would be a good idea for both of them to do a lot of thinking instead of talking on the way to the club so their minds would be prepared to make sensible decisions. As they walked up Union Street, several people spoke to them but, instead of stopping to talk, they merely waved a friendly greeting each time.

There had not been a word spoken by either of them until they got to the club and sat down at a table in the far corner of the bar. This was when Ben ordered two sundowners. Nothing more was said after that until the two double-bourbon-and-single-water drinks had been brought to the table.

"I suppose you heard about Willy Shoelong, the so-called Memphis barber, getting it good and plenty in police court this morning," Ben remarked in a casual manner after both of them had taken a drink. He was confident that he could persuade Grover to act on his advice, but he wanted to delay further talk about the matter until he was sure of the best way to go about it. "Willy started out talking big like he was running the court himself and demanded to have his own lawyer from Memphis, but Judge Painter already had his own ideas about that. He appointed one of the local lawyers who happened to be in court to represent Willy. And that was the end of it. Willy got the maximum as fast as Judge Painter could throw it at him. A year at hard labor for pulling a knife on the two Wolverton policemen who arrested him for speeding."

Grover reached for his glass and gulped down the drink.

"There's no chance of Willy Shoelong getting out on a bail bond now, is there, Ben?" he asked hurriedly, almost upsetting the empty glass as he was putting it on the table.

"No. Why?"

"I was just wondering—that's all."

"You've got the shakes real bad, bub. What you need to cure that is another fast drink."

Ben rattled the ice cubes in his glass and loudly called for two more sundowners. They sat in silence until they had been served the second round of drinks.

Carefully lowering his voice so that the other men in the bar could not overhear what was said, Ben leaned over the table.

"I'm going to tell you something now, Grover, and I've thought about it very carefully. And don't you say anything till I finish what I want to say. You'll have your turn. Now, it's like this. I want you to put off for one solid year the whole idea of wanting to marry that colored

58

girl and then at the end of a year we'll talk about it again if necessary. And for one solid year you can keep her, like I said back at the office. You'll be a lot better off with none of the trouble. And the only difference between marrying her and keeping her will be that you've got to make sure you won't be seen with her by anybody—black or white—anytime, anywhere. Absolutely not! Do you understand?"

Grover nodded. "I hear you, but—"

"Wait till I finish, Grover," he said sharply. "Now, here's what it is. You can see her as much as you want at your house after your help has gone home for the night and before they come back to work in the morning. Or when you want to give Annie and Della a day off. There you are! What more could you ask for—married or not? Now, you think about that and see if you don't come up with the same way of thinking as I do."

Grover picked up his glass and leaned all the way back in his chair. He sat there staring across the room as if he were looking at a hazy landmark miles away.

"Well?" Ben said presently, impatiently rapping on the table with his knuckles. "What about it, Grover?"

"How could I do that, Ben? If I went for her, she couldn't ride with me through town without being seen by somebody. And it's too far for her to walk all the way from Wolverton to my house and back."

"Simple, bub. Very simple. I was waiting for you to say that. You'll buy her an automobile. Not a brand-new one, though. That would get too much attention. But a good reliable used car that looks like one a schoolteacher could afford. It will have to be a nice conservative color, too—no bright red or anything like that. And it'll be licensed in her name, not yours. And the insurance in her name, too. You'll pay for everything. See how it's working out now? And I'll take care of all the details for you. That's the only way it can be, bub. But the next time you get a notion about a woman be sure to pick out a white girl for it—or else get yourself another lawyer. You hear?"

"I hear."

"And when I say a white girl, I don't mean Gladys. You hear?"

"I hear."

Chapter

SIX

In the sweltering afternoons of August during the past several years when he was on his way home at six o'clock after finishing work at the stables for the day, Jeff Bazemore had been in the habit of stopping at the freshwater pond near the lower fencing of the pony farm to go swimming alone for half an hour or longer.

The few times Jeff had not stopped to swim in the pond were when there was a violent summer thunder and lightning storm in late afternoon and then he always went straight home to the Lawson house in Halfway Hollow.

Although by that time the pond had not been used for watering the Shetlands for many years, and it had become surrounded by tall oaks and bushy willow undergrowth that kept it from being visible from the railroad tracks, the well-trodden wide path the ponies had made from the weather shelter was still not overgrown with stubble and saplings and Jeff was in the habit of undressing in the shelter and leaving his clothes there when he went down the path to go swimming. He had never asked Grover Danford or Jim Whittaker for permission to swim in the pond and he had never thought that anybody knew he ever went there.

The other stable boys had shorter ways of going home since they lived in different directions and Jeff had become accustomed to being alone and he liked to think of the pond being his own private swimming pool. As the summer days became hotter and more humid, each time he ran splashing in the cool clear water he hoped that someday he could have a pony farm of his own with a big pond to swim in.

Jeff Bazemore was sixteen years old that summer with one more year of high school to complete before leaving home to enter college. Grover Danford had assured him several times during the past year that he was going to have a four-year college education with all expenses paid as a bonus for having worked so hard and faithfully since he began helping train the Shetlands when he was nine years old.

Already six feet in height and sturdy in body, Jeff had grown up during the past year to be a handsome young man with wavy brown hair and coloring of skin even lighter than had been the pale brownness of his mother. When Grover and Jeff happened to be together at the paddocks and stables, they had a noticeable resemblance particularly in the shape of their slender noses and the molding of their lips and a pronounced arching of their eyebrows. Several times in recent months Jim Whittaker had remarked in a seemingly casual manner, but never within Grover's hearing, that they looked so much alike that anybody who did not know who they were might think they were closely related.

It was one of the usual sweltering afternoons of August when Jeff, after swimming and splashing in the pond for nearly an hour that day, waded out of the water and went up the pony path to the weather shelter to put on his clothes.

The day had been cloudless with no threat of a thunderstorm, but by that time in the afternoon with the sun still far from setting, the air was becoming cool and comfortable in the shade and shadows. Unhurried, and lazily whistling occasionally, Jeff took his time as he went up the grassy path. Supper at the Lawson house was always after sundown in summer and winter alike and there were nearly two hours of daylight left.

When Jeff got to the shelter, his clothes were no longer on the bench where he knew he had left them nor were they anywhere within sight. He knew the exact spot where he had left his shirt and pants when he undressed, because he always put them at the same place each time, and his immediate thought was that one of the other stable boys was playing a joke on him by hiding his clothes while he was at the pond. He was not particularly worried at first, because there were not many places under the weather shelter where anything like that could be put out of sight.

While trying to think which one of his friends would be most likely to play that kind of joke on him, he started looking for places where his shirt and pants and shoes might be hidden. He looked first in the horse stall, then in all the feed racks, overhead in the rafters, and finally went behind the tall stack of baled hay that was kept in the rear part of the shelter.

Still not finding his clothes, Jeff turned around to look for them somewhere else, and that was when he saw

Effie Devlin standing in the narrow passageway between the shelter wall and the stack of baled hay.

Even though he was too surprised to say anything, he knew he was cornered with no way of escape as long as she stood there.

Suddenly becoming embarrassed as he realized that she was seeing him completely naked, he hunched his shoulders forward and tried to cover himself with his hands as much as possible.

As he stared at her, he wondered why Effie Devlin would come to the weather shelter and hide his clothes.

"Hello, Jeff," he heard her saying.

He nodded to her without saying a word.

"Don't you know who I am, Jeff?"

He nodded again.

"Then don't stand there acting so scared looking," Effie, her voice sounding husky and excited, said with a brief smile. "You don't have to be scared of nothing. You can act natural. Nobody knows about it."

"Nobody knows about what?" he asked fearfully.

"Nobody knows I followed you down here."

"What did you do that for?"

"Why you reckon?"

"I don't know but I wish you hadn't done it."

"Jeff, you don't want to say that and hurt my feelings, do you?"

She had moved a step closer and was smiling at him with a slight shaking of her head.

"You hid my clothes, didn't you?" he said accusingly. "What made you do that?"

"So you couldn't run off—that's why. My goodness, you look real handsome! You sure growed up a lot this summer. My goodness! How old are you, Jeff?"

He was shaking his head worriedly. "Sixteen. But I can't stay here like this. Mrs. Devlin, please give me my clothes back now and let me go. Please ma'am, will you do that? Where did you hide them?"

Instead of answering him, Effie began shaking dust and cobwebs from an old brown saddlecloth she had been holding. Jeff recognized it immediately, because he had seen it hanging all summer on a peg near the horse stall.

Although he was curious about why she would be shaking dust from the saddlecloth, he was more concerned then about getting his clothes and covering himself than anything else. Effie continued shaking the saddlecloth energetically, as if determined to dislodge the last speck of dust and cobweb.

"Please ma'am, tell me where you hid my clothes," he pleaded. "Mrs. Devlin, I don't want to get in trouble—trouble like this—this kind of way. I'm a colored boy and—"

"There won't be no trouble about nothing now or no other time if you act right," she told him in a soothing voice.

"What's right—the way you said it?"

"My goodness, you know how to do right. You couldn't grow up big like you are now and not know about that."

"But what do you want me to do?"

"My goodness! Now ain't that another funny question!"

"Maybe it sounds like that to you, Mrs. Devlin, but it's serious to me."

Jeff had been trying to keep himself covered the best he could with his hands and arms, and then suddenly he reached desperately for the saddlecloth to wrap around himself. Effie jerked it out of his reach before he could get his hand on it, and then, smiling excitedly, she began unfastening her dress. She had already taken off her shoes, and as the faded green dress dropped at her feet he saw that it was her only clothing. Tossing her tangled short blond hair away from her face, she stood there with the whiteness of her naked body gleaming boldly in the faint light of the afternoon sun.

II

Effie Devlin was a large woman with thick arms and legs and great heavy buttocks and, although she was only in her early twenties, her bulging weight made her look at least ten years older than she actually was. Lumps of fat on her hips made puffy swellings under her skin and her huge breasts hung downward as if heavily weighted and swayed from side to side with the slightest movement of her body. She had a round-faced pleasant smile and there were small dimples in her cheeks, but she had several jagged and darkly discolored teeth that gave her a menacing appearance even when she was smilingly pleased about something. Effie had been married for several years to Mike Devlin, who had been one of Grover Danford's truck drivers for a long time, and they lived in one of the small white cottages beside Saddle Creek.

Mike and Effie had been having frequent noisy quarrels ever since they were married and there had been times when they left the house and went to the front yard to shout and scrap and tumble on the ground in full view of the neighbors. Even though they were just about the same in height, Effie was much heavier than Mike and usually succeeded in holding him on the ground and beating him with her fists and battering him with elbows and knees until he was willing to give up and quit. After one of their slambang fights they would go back into the house and Effie would be jolly and loving for the next several days until the next quarrel began.

When Mike was asked what he and Effie quarreled so much about, he said that Effie always started it by complaining that he drank more than his share of beer when he brought home a few bottles on Saturday night. Effie, however, said the true reason was because there were many times when he got a paycheck from Grover Danford that he saved it to take on a trucking trip and cashed it in a whorehouse in Memphis or some other place he went instead of giving her some of the money for cooking his meals and sleeping with him.

"Mrs. Devlin, I've just got to go," Jeff pleaded with her desperately. "Don't make me stay here any longer like this. Please tell me where you hid my clothes. Just my pants will do. You can keep the rest if you want to. I can't go home through town naked like this. The police would get me for sure. They'd lock me up in jail. I don't want that kind of trouble. Please, ma'am, let me go."

"My goodness, Jeff, take it easy. You don't have to go nowhere now. Nobody's coming poking around this old weather shelter and peeping on us. Except maybe some ponies and they don't count. Right here's the safest place to be in the whole country. You take my word for it. I ain't scared and there ain't nothing for you to be scared about."

"Mrs. Devlin—I can't help it. Maybe it's all right for you not to be scared, but I can't help it."

Effie giggled.

"If that mister cocker of yours could talk, it wouldn't be saying nothing like that. It ain't scared one bit. I can tell by the way it's acting up. It's real pleased and begging to stay. You pay mind to what it wants and you won't go off."

"But, Mrs. Devlin—you're a white lady and—"

"You could almost pass for white yourself, Jeff. My goodness, you don't even look nowhere near half colored or nothing like that. You've got that pretty wavy brown hair and no real blackness on you nowhere at all. What are you, anyhow? Are you part Indian or Gypsy along

64

with some white too? How did you get to be born looking like you do?"

"I don't know about that, but—"

"If you're scared of Mike—if that's what's bothering you—Mike ain't nowhere near here for you to worry about. He'll be gone for two or three whole days. He went off taking a truckload of ponies all the way to St. Louis."

"I know—I helped load the ponies yesterday morning. But that makes no difference. I want my clothes, Mrs. Devlin. Please move out of the way and let me go look for them myself."

Effie reached down for the faded brown saddlecloth and shook some more dust from it.

"You quit that acting now like a mean old stranger man." She pouted with an annoyed toss of her tangled blond hair. "You've seen me plenty of times before around the stables. I've watched you plenty of times up there, too. I've been watching you and getting a notion even if you didn't know it. And I followed you down here yesterday afternoon when you went swimming in the pond. I figured that was the right time after Mike had gone off to St. Louis, and I was hiding in the bushes watching you and waiting for you to finish. But something must've scared you—maybe you heard me or saw me in the bushes—because you left in a hurry and ran up here to the shelter and got dressed so fast I couldn't get here in time to stop you before you left. That's why I came back down here today and hid your clothes from you and they're going to stay hid, too, till you act right."

Jeff moved uneasily, shifting his weight from one leg to the other several times. As he looked at Effie Devlin then, her large body seemed to have expanded until it completely blocked the narrow passage between the shelter wall and the high stack of baled hay.

"My goodness, you look like you're getting all ready to act right." Effie said with a pleased smile. "You might be scared, but mister cocker sure ain't showing no signs of it."

"What do you want me to do, Mrs. Devlin?"

Effie stooped over and carefully spread the saddlecloth on the splintery flooring.

"Throw me, big boy! I want to be throwed!"

She had straightened up and was standing on the saddlecloth with a parting of her legs. Her round face was flushed with excitement and small beads of sweat glistened on her stomach as her fleshy body began rocking back and forth.

"I'm telling you right," Effie said with an impatient frown, "if you don't hurry up and throw me, I'm going to throw you. My goodness, I didn't come down here twice—both yesterday and this time—for a lot of nothing. Not after watching and waiting all summer, too. I've got my pride. Now come here closer and I'll diddle you some first. I'll make it easy for you. I know how. That mister cocker's all ready to get started. It's got a whopper of a jump on and it knows where miss purdy is. Sick 'em, mister cocker!"

"Mrs. Devlin—if anybody saw me—Mrs. Devlin!"

"Sick'em, mister cocker! Go for miss purdy!"

Effie moved a step closer to Jeff, and then as she reached for him, he made a headlong lunge toward the narrow passage in a desperate effort to get away from her.

Watchful and alert, Effie instantly locked her strong arms around his waist and lifted him until his feet were dangling above the floor. Crushed tightly in her arms, he was struggling to breathe when she bit his shoulder so painfully with her jagged teeth that he yelled and tried to free himself with jabbings of his elbows. Squeezing him more tightly, Effie did not stop biting him until he had yelled loudly the second time and then she threw him backward on the saddlecloth. The weight of her body falling on him had made him completely breathless and while he was struggling to get his breath back she was already sitting upright on him and straddling his thighs with a powerful grip of her legs.

"My goodness, just act natural, mister cocker," Effie said with a husky tenderness.

Then, holding her breath momentarily, she covered him with a sudden thrust of her body.

"Now make yourself at home, mister cocker," she whispered. "You're welcome. Don't be bashful."

Almost immediately she began beating his chest and shoulders with her fists. When he could endure the painful pounding no longer, Jeff tried to shove her away with his arms and elbows, but nothing would make her stop hurting him until he reached up and grasped her huge breasts as they swung above him. Her breasts were too large to be held completely in his hands and he had to dig his fingernails into her flesh in order to keep part of them in his grasp. Effie, not hitting him again a single time after that, began smiling contentedly. Sweat was running down her

neck and breasts and dripping on him and he could taste
the salt of it in his mouth.

III

Her round face flushed and glowing, and still smiling happily, Effie tossed her blond hair backward and began
singing.

> *Every day in the morning*
> *When I first wake up,*
> *I ain't a bit happy*
> *Till I can go—hup!*

By the time she had reached the end of the verse, she
had slowly raised herself upward on her knees, and that
was when she suddenly thrust downward upon him with
the full weight of her body.

"My goodness! Ain't that a pretty song?" she said, sigh-
ing deeply and looking down at him with her glowing
smile. "It's the exact right kind to fit the occasion, ain't
it, Jeff? I don't know how long ago it was when I heard it
first—maybe it just came to me and I made it up myself.
I like to do things like that. Anyhow, it gets prettier and
suits real natural everytime I sing it like that. You learn
it from me now so you can sing it and you'll think so,
too."

With no will to resist her any longer, and forgetting all
his fear, Jeff grasped her huge breasts more eagerly.

Closing her eyes, and with an elated toss of her head,
Effie began singing again.

> *If the bright old sun don't shine*
> *And make me get up,*
> *That's the bestest time then*
> *For some more—hup! hup!*

At the end, Effie thrust herself downward on him twice
with the full weight of her body.

"That ain't all of the song," she was saying. "There's
some more of it. My goodness, I never want to stop after
I get started!"

Her body had continued to sway with the musical beat
when she began singing again.

> *After the sun goes down*
> *And the moon comes up,*

67

It's never much like me
To waste that time—wup!

Effie finished singing the verse with another excited thrust of her body.

"You sing along with me this time," she told Jeff as she began bouncing up and down with the rhythm of the song. "Come on and sing, Jeff. You'll catch on to all the words—it's easy to do. And you do some hupping and wupping, too. Both of us'll do it at the same time. My goodness, that'll make it even better!"

His hands slippery with sweat in the summer heat, Jeff could no longer keep her breasts in his grasp as Effie started singing and shaking with the musical beat, and he reached as far around her as he could and dug his finger-nails into the warm flesh of her buttocks.

If it's middle of the night
When I'm waking up,
What I always do first
I start to like—wup! wup!

Effie had begun singing another verse, but after the first few words she stopped abruptly as if she had suddenly become spent and exhausted. With a heave and a sigh as she tumbled, she lay sprawling wearily on the hard floor beside him.

"Are you all right, Mrs. Devlin?" Jeff asked as he sat upright and looked down at her, fearful that she was having a heart attack and would die right there. "Mrs. Devlin —Mrs. Devlin—what's the matter? Say something! What's wrong with you, Mrs. Devlin?"

Without opening her eyes, Effie smiled slightly as she took a long deep breath.

"Nothing's wrong at all," she said after a moment. "I didn't want to quit sooner but I got all tired out all of a sudden. My goodness, you sure outlasted me. It wasn't your fault to have to quit."

Slowly opening her eyes, she looked up at Jeff then.

"Now I'll tell you where I hid your clothes. Go look behind that stack of hay over there where it leans against the wall. I bet you could've looked a whole day and never found that secret hiding place."

After getting his clothes and hurriedly dressing, he came back to where Effie was sitting up and putting on her shoes. While he was watching her and wondering why she was putting on her shoes before putting on her dress, she looked up and smiled.

"Jeff, ain't you glad now you didn't get away like you tried to do a while ago? Now ain't you really?"

Suddenly reminded of how fearful he had been that somebody would see him with her, he looked around the weather shelter with a worried glance.

"Mrs. Devlin—I—I've got to go!"

"My goodness, don't hurry off yet, Jeff. I'd feel lonesome. Stay a while longer and keep me company. And that's such a pretty song I want to keep on singing it. My goodness, let's start at the beginning and sing it some more."

Closing her eyes, and her huge breasts swinging rhythmically, she began singing.

> *Every day in the morning*
> *When I first wake up,*
> *I ain't a bit happy*
> *Till I can go—hup!*

As she was finishing the first verse, she tried to bounce her heavy buttocks up and down but she was unable to lift her body from the floor. With a weary sigh, she began struggling to get up, and Jeff grasped one of her arms with both hands and pulled until she could get to her feet.

"I'm so glad you ain't mad at me now and I'm a heap gladder than that myself for personal reasons you don't know about," she told him as she began brushing his shirt and pants with sweeping strokes of her hands.

He could see tears in her eyes and he wondered why she would be crying after saying she was so pleased.

"My goodness, Jeff, just look there at that old dust and nasty spider webs on your nice clothes. I don't want you going home looking like that—it'd make me ashamed about it. It's all my fault for not finding a better hiding place—but I was in such a big rush to get your clothes hid from you that I didn't know half of what I was doing. I'm so ashamed of myself about that. I want you to look nice in your clothes."

When she finally finished brushing his shirt and pants to her satisfaction, she stepped back and nodded approvingly. After that she picked up her faded green dress and shook some of the wrinkles from it.

"You want to know something, Jeff?"

"What is it, Mrs. Devlin?"

"It's a secret, but I'll tell you why I'm so glad—if you

won't tell anybody about it." Tears were running down her flushed face as she put on her dress. "I want you to know—but you'll have to promise not to tell."

"I won't tell anybody, Mrs. Devlin," he said at once. "Honest, I won't."

"Then don't never let Mike know about it. He'd beat the life out of me till he made me tell who done it. Then he'd be after you, too."

Tears were running down her face faster than she could wipe them away.

"Ever since I got married to Mike—all this time—I've wanted a real live baby of my own. But Mike can't give it to me. There's something wrong with him that way—he keeps on doing everything about it but a baby never comes. I went to the doctor and he said there's nothing wrong with me and that it's Mike's fault and none of mine. Just one baby would be enough if I couldn't get more. Just only one would do. I've prayed and prayed and tried and tried and swallowed cookstove ashes and chewed sassafras roots but nothing helps. There's a man— a white man—who works here on the pony farm. But he wouldn't have nothing to do with me. He said I was too big and fat for him to fool with. That was about two months ago. And after that was when I picked you out and started watching you and thinking about how to go about it. You're white enough. That won't make no difference. You don't look nowhere colored to me. And now I'm going to have a baby—I just know it—I just know I am!"

Jeff, stunned, and feeling too weak to stand, sat down on a bale of hay. He had never thought of anything like that happening to him—not even with a colored girl— and a sensation of numbness came over him as he stared at Effie's whiteness of skin with the fearful realization of what she had said.

Effie had got down on her knees and was pressing her damp face against him as she hugged him with all the strength of her arms. She had almost stopped crying then and her trembling and sobbing gradually vanished as she clung to him.

"My goodness, I'm so happy now," Jeff could hear her saying barely above a whisper as though she were talking to herself. "And you done it to make me so happy. I'm going to have a precious little baby to cuddle and nurse and take care of. It's what I've been wanting so long and couldn't get. I've got dozens of pretty dolls to play with —I made a lot of them myself. My goodness, I've got so many dolls I can't always remember all their names and have to stop and think about it before I can play with them sometimes. But as soon as I start playing with them it makes me feel worse because they ain't real and that makes me cry my eyes out."

Effie raised her head and looked up at Jeff.

"Now I won't have to cry like that no more—I'll know my own precious real little baby doll is coming. I won't never have to play with make-believe babies and cry my eyes out after that. I wish I'd followed you down here to the weather shelter a lot sooner and then I wouldn't have to wait that much longer for my precious little real baby. I'm so happy now I'm going to cry some, anyhow."

SEVEN

When Grover Danford heard about the threats that had been made by Mike Devlin, it was the middle of the afternoon of a mild and pleasant early June day.

It was nothing new for Mike to lose his temper over some trivial remark or incident and get into a fistfight in Wolverton or anywhere else, but he had never been heard to threaten to kill anybody before. Several times he had been locked up overnight in the city jail and fined ten dollars in police court the next morning for being drunk and creating a disturbance on Union Street, but he had never been charged with an offense more serious than that. He was a burly, hard-muscled man with bristly black hair and a broad flat face who liked to show off his strength when he had a few drinks and would boast that it always took three policemen and two blackjacks to get handcuffs on him.

Grover and Jim Whittaker had been in the stable office going over business accounts for about half an hour and Jim had waited until the business matters had been finished before telling Grover what had happened at the stables earlier that afternoon.

What had happened was that Mike Devlin had taken the small pickup truck to the feed mill in Wolverton for the usual weekly load of sacked oats and shelled corn and when he got back he yelled for the stable boys to hurry up and carry the sacks of pony feed into the barn. Even though Jeff Bazemore was the first one to get there, Mike cursed him for not getting there faster and shoved him against the side of the truck with such force that Jeff lost his balance and fell to the ground.

It was when Jeff was getting up that Mike told him that he would be lucky to have one chance out of a hundred to be alive and on his feet another time to unload pony feed or anything else. Jeff had been too frightened to say a word then and was even more frightened when Mike followed him into the barn and told him that if he knew what was going to happen to him he would start running right then for his life while he could.

Even though he had been there all the time and had seen the shoving and heard the threats, Jim said he was so worried that he decided not to say anything for fear of aggravating Mike and making him so angry that he might come back that night and set fire to the barns and stables. Instead, he had sent Jeff off on a saddle horse to the north pasture and told him to stay there with the Shetlands until he was sent for later in the day.

Jeff, seventeen years old then, had graduated from high school the week before and had already been accepted and enrolled at the college in Nashville he expected to enter at the end of summer.

Early in May, several weeks before graduation, one of the other stable boys had told Jeff that Effie Devlin gave birth to a baby whose coloring and facial features were so unlike Mike's that he was suspicious and had warned Effie that he was going to keep after her day and night and not quit until she told him who the baby's father was. None of the neighbors had actually seen Mike beating Effie to make her tell, but, as some of them said, they had often heard her screams and his angry yelling and the sound of chairs and tables splintering as they were hurled against the walls of the small cottage on Saddle Creek.

When Jeff heard about Effie Devlin's baby the first time, he remembered clearly what she had said at the weather shelter that afternoon in the previous summer, but that seemed to him then to be so far in the past that he could not believe he would be the father of the baby. Recently, however, he heard a stable boy tell another one that the baby looked more like Jeff than Mike Devlin and then he was really worried.

"What do you think we'd better do?" Grover asked when Jim finished telling about what had happened earlier in the afternoon. He got up from his office chair and began walking nervously back and forth. "What's best, Jim? Give Mike Devlin a month's pay and get him away from here as fast as we can?"

"That wouldn't stop Mike not for one minute, Grover. Even if we paid him off and told him to move away, he'd still be likely to stay around Wolverton and could go after that boy. When somebody like him gets that kind of grudge, he's not apt to be pacified that easy. It's because of that baby his wife had about a month ago. That's what it's all about. You've heard as much gossip as anybody else. The way I figure it, Mike Devlin finally made Effie

73

talk—just like he's been boasting he was going to do. I don't know what he done to make her talk—but I could make a safe guess."

"I know," Grover said gravely. He went to the window and stood there gazing thoughtfully at the empty paddocks for a while. "I know," he said again when he turned and looked at Jim. "I've been afraid of this ever since I heard about that baby—the coloring and the resemblance—"

Jim nodded.

"Jim, I don't know the truth about it and I've held off saying the first word about it to Jeff. But—but if what I've heard is true—"

"Grover, you might as well go ahead and make up your mind to let yourself believe it." Jim was speaking in a quietly serious tone of voice. "What's done is done and you can't change what is."

Grover was shaking his head. "It's hard for me to believe Jeff, at his age, would rape a white woman. He was only sixteen last summer—when this took place—if it actually did at all—and he's still only a boy even now."

"There's more than one way, Grover. You know that. I wouldn't want to try to make myself believe that it had to be a raping that made Effie Devlin come to have a baby looking like him. But one way or the other, it don't make a goddam bit of difference at all now. It's done. I remember watching Effie Devlin hanging around the paddocks last summer and I'd have been as blind as a chicken with its head cut off not to know what she was after. She was looking for a pronging—I know the signs when I see them. And you can't put the blame on a young boy like Jeff Bazemore when she set out to make it so easy for him."

"I noticed her hanging around, too, but I thought she'd stay with her own color."

"Both of us are wasting time doing all this talking about the past and it's right now to worry about, Grover. You'd better get that boy as far away from here as you can and as fast as you can. And I mean far and fast right away. If he's here much after sundown tonight, I wouldn't count on him being alive at sunup tomorrow morning. That's how serious it is. If you'd heard the way Mike Devlin was talking—well, take my advice, Grover, and get the boy away from here in a goddam hurry. Don't waste time. I'd hate to see the worst happen to him."

"I'll have to try to think of the best place to take him where somebody I can trust would be sure to watch out

74

for him. Somebody like Mary and Pete Lawson. I don't know anybody like that in Memphis or Nashville. And I wouldn't want to board him with strangers who might not take good care of him. He's still just a young boy and I—"

"Well, you'd better start thinking and figuring right away. You know yourself there's too goddam many night riders around Wolverton and all over Wolver County for comfort and Mike's real chummy with those people. And it only takes a few telephone calls and some grapevining and a little trip here and there to get a whole crowd of them stirred up. I know a lot of them by name and heard them talk the way they do. This's the kind of thing they like to wait around for to happen—a colored man and a white woman—and they can crank up and start their night-riding as soon as the sun goes down. Mike's gone from here already—he said he had to take the rest of the day off from work to attend to something and that's a bad sign right there to begin with."

The long brass pendulum of the big clock on the wall seemed to have speeded up and started ticking faster and faster. Jim, getting up from his chair, crossed the room and stood with his back against the door.

"Grover, I've always watched my talk around you and never asked you outright in plain words, and you've never let on about it, but I know Jeff is your natural son just as well as you know it—and the same way like me and you both know who his mother was, too. There's nothing about that to hide between me and you now. I knew all about you and her down there at the weather shelter on Sundays and up there in your house some nights and everywhere else right up to the time she got shot to death. I never did no snooping around. That's not my nature. The way it was, everything was as plain as broad daylight for me to see. But I keep what I know to myself and always will.

"Well, that's all I'm going to say about that. But what I am going to say now is that if he was a son of mine—no matter if I'm white and he's got color—but no matter, I'd do exactly like you're going to do to keep him from getting his balls butchered off or shot to death by the night riders. They'd go after him like it was a turkey shoot in a cow pasture the day before Thanksgiving—or like me and you would geld a colt. Now get goddam busy about it, Grover, and start figuring how you're going to get him away from here by dark tonight and where you're going to take him to."

"Jeff's got grandparents in Tupelo," Grover spoke up.

A slight smile of relief quickly came to his face. "I remember now. His mother's parents lived there—I hope they're still alive and living in Tupelo. I'll find them somehow—I've got to—I can get there tonight."

"All right, but there's no time left to waste," Jim told him. "What reason are you going to tell your wife for going off like this with Jeff?"

"I won't have to tell her anything. Madge has been in Nashville for the past four days and I don't know when she'll be back."

"Well, that does save the trouble of figuring out a good excuse to tell her. And while we just happen to be talking about her, if I was pinned down and made to come right out and say it in plain words—"

"Go ahead, Jim," Grover told him approvingly. "It's all right. Say anything you want to."

"Well, I know it ain't right for no man to talk about another man's wife the way I'm thinking. But, goddam it, Grover, I've waited long enough to speak out again like I want to and there's no better time to say it than now like this. I don't remember how many years you've been married to her—except I do know it's been too goddam long for any man to put up with and don't even have one son by her to show for it. I don't know the reason—and you can tell me it's none of my goddam business—but you've proved it can be done. Anyhow, she's not giving you a son to grow up and run this pony farm like it ought to be when it's your time to go. I know this ain't the first time you've heard me say it, but—"

"That's a personal matter between Madge and me, Jim. But I'll tell you this much. She said even before we were married a doctor in Nashville was giving her special treatments for a certain physical condition and that it takes a long time for a complete cure."

"I can't doubt that there's something wrong, but it sounds like she's got a peculiar kind of female trouble to take so long to cure. And so she's still taking the treatments after all this time?"

Grover said that was what he was told.

"Well, maybe so," Jim remarked with a doubtful frown. "But it don't sound good to me. I never did believe in all the mysterious female troubles I've heard about. And the fact remains. Your daddy left a son when he went and it would be a goddam shame for you not to do likewise. It just ain't natural for a man not to want to have a son to leave behind. And now I'll tell you something that even surprised my own self when I thought about it. I've always been against race mixing and still am as a rule. But somehow it makes a difference when it comes this close to home. I've been with your daddy and you nearly all my life and feel like one of the family now."

Jim paused and glanced aside for a moment. He swallowed hard before speaking again.

"Grover, maybe that's why I don't want to see no harm come to a son of yours even if he does have mixed blood —and likely to be the only son you'll ever have. I think the world of this pony farm, just like it was my own, and I don't want to see a woman like her getting it all for herself when she don't deserve one single little fence post of it. That's why I want to see you go ahead right away and take good care of the one son you've got. That's right, Grover. I mean it. I know it don't sound like me ordinarily, but I mean it now. Then after you've taken good care of him and got him out of harm, start figuring on getting rid of a woman you've had to put up with all this time for nothing. I ain't at all convinced a contrary woman like her even goes to bed with you to take care of your ordinary wants when she's here—and she ain't here nine time out of ten, anyhow."

Grover put on his hat and went toward the door.

"That's something for me to think about some other time, Jim. I mean, about her. That can wait. Right now I want to get Jeff away from here."

When they got outside, the sun was already so low in the sky that it looked as if it would be setting within half an hour. Jim immediately told one of the stable boys to saddle a horse as fast as he could and ride to the north pasture to tell Jeff to hurry back to the stables.

II

After Grover had driven his large dark blue sedan from the garage and left it in the driveway with the engine running, he noticed a tensely worried expression on Jim Whittaker's lean tanned face.

That was when Jim said it would be too dangerous for Jeff to be seen riding through Wolverton in the car, or even trying to crouch out of sight in the rear seat and going roundabout on a back road, and that the only safe way of getting him to Tupelo that night would be to have him ride in the trunk and stay there at least until they had gone several miles beyond Wolverton. The only way to avoid going through Wolverton, as they knew, was to take a little-used dirt road that made a wide circle around the town and joined the main highway several miles to the south near Bushy Creek.

Grover agreed at once that it was a wise precaution to take. While he was getting a thin cot mattress to put into the trunk for Jeff to lie on, Jim got a hacksaw from the shop and cut an opening in the metal flooring large enough to give Jeff sufficient fresh air as long as he had to stay locked in the trunk.

As they were waiting for Jeff to get there, Jim said he would go to Wolverton later in the evening and tell Pete and Mary Lawson not to worry about Jeff's not coming home that night and to explain that he had been sent away on a trip out of town for a while. He said he would try to assure them that Jeff would be safe where he was as long as he was away from home and, also, warn the Lawsons not to say anything more than that about it if somebody came to their house and tried to find out if they knew where Jeff was.

It was sunset when Jeff got back to the stables and was told what was going to be done. He was too frightened to say much when Grover explained that he was worried about Mike Devlin's threats and that they had to get away from Wolverton before there was a chance of anything harmful happening to him. As Jeff was climbing into the trunk of the car, Grover told him not to make a sound of any kind if they had to stop along the road and somebody pounded on the trunk and called him by name. Grover said he would unlock the trunk just as soon as he was sure they had gone far enough from Wolverton for it to be safe for him to get out and ride in the front seat.

"What would they do to me, Mr. Grover?" Jeff asked fearfully with a trembling of his lips. There were no tears visible, but his eyes blinked as he tried to hold them back. "Mr. Grover—what would they do?"

"We don't know, Jeff, and we don't want to think about it now."

"I'm scared, Mr. Grover."

"I know. But I'm going to take care of you."

Jeff held his hand upward against the lid of the trunk to keep Grover from closing it.

"Mr. Grover, I couldn't help what happened last summer. It was down there at the weather shelter after I'd gone swimming in the pond. Mrs. Devlin—she hid my clothes and wouldn't give them back. I tried to get away from her, anyhow, but couldn't. She was too big and strong. That's the truth, Mr. Grover. I wouldn't try to make a white lady do that. I know better. But she wouldn't let me go and then after that I couldn't help myself. It was like wanting—wanting to do what she wanted then."

"I know, Jeff. I understand. We can talk about it again some other time. Right now we've got to go."

Jeff lay down on the mattress and drew his knees up against his chest in order to fit himself into the length of the trunk. The trunk of the big sedan was spacious enough in height and width so he could turn over and move around whenever he wanted to, but he would have to keep his knees doubled up all the time he was there.

"Where are we going, Mr. Grover?" he asked.

"Down to Tupelo to look for your Bazemore grandparents so you can stay with them for a while."

"I've never seen them. Do they know who I am?"

"They'll know when I tell them."

"Papa and Mama Lawson won't know where I went. I want to let them know so they won't be worried about me."

"That'll be taken care of tonight. Jim Whittaker is going down there to see them."

"But I need to go by home and get some of my clothes if I'm going to be gone a while. I've got some better pants than these, and some clean shirts, too. And I could see Papa and Mama before I left."

"No, Jeff. We can't do that. I'm sorry. But we can't risk it. We're not going anywhere near the Lawson house. We're not even going through Wolverton—we're going miles around it. But don't worry about clothes. We'll get some new clothes for you in Tupelo."

"If nothing bad happens—Mr. Grover—will I still be going off to college like you said I could?"

"Yes. You'll be going. But right now there's something more important to think about. Now keep your head down while I slam this trunk shut. And don't forget what I told you about keeping quiet and not saying a word, not even to me, no matter what happens, until I unlock the trunk."

"I won't forget. And there's just one thing I want to say before you lock me in here."

"What is it?"

"Mr. Grover—I'm so glad you want to look out for me like you're doing."

"It's what I want to do, Jeff. And I always will. You can count on that."

After closing the trunk and testing it to make sure that

it was locked securely, Grover got into the sedan to leave. Just before he drove off into the dwindling twilight, Jim Whittaker warned him about driving too fast on the narrow country road and reminded him of the deep ditches on both sides of it. It had not rained for the past several days and the surface of the dirt road was dry and slightly dusty. However, as usual in summer and winter, there was standing water in some of the deep ditches and flooded dips in the road where banks were slippery with mud.

III

Darkness, as usual at that time of year, was coming rapidly as Grover turned the car into the narrow dirt road. A full moon was rising over the highland rim; however, it was too soon for the moon to give enough light to see by and Grover knew it would not be long until he would have to switch on the headlights. Even though there were very few farmhouses along the isolated road, he wanted to go as far as possible before anybody saw the headlights of an automobile coming from the pony farm and going southward on the back-country road at that time of evening. There were telephones in some of the farmhouses and word could be spread widely within a few minutes.

When at last it became too dark to drive without the danger of running off the road and getting bogged down in a ditch, Grover finally turned on the headlights. He had gone several miles by then and he could tell by looking at the familiar pine groves and cultivated fields along the roadside that he was only about a quarter of a mile from the paved highway and would soon be able to speed up the car and get farther away from Wolverton. He had neither seen anybody along the road nor had he met a single car since leaving the stables. Also, it was a relief to know, having frequently glanced at the rear-view mirror, that so far he was not being followed by anybody in another automobile.

Coming to the end of the dirt road, Grover stopped the sedan momentarily before turning southward on the paved highway and looked backward at the glow of moonlight over Wolverton. The town was only a short distance away and the moon by then had risen high enough to reveal the rusty tin-roofed dome of the county courthouse and the needle-pointed white steeple of the Trinity Baptist Church.

Now that he was safely on the other side of Wolverton,

he wondered if it had been necessary to waste so much time driving slowly over the rough road and going several miles out of the way to avoid driving through the town. Tupelo was still almost as far away as ever and he knew he was going to be uneasy and apprehensive every minite until he could get all the way there with Jeff.

Grover began driving rapidly toward Tupelo and after going about a mile had crossed the bridge over Bushy Creek. Less than a hundred yards beyond the bridge there was a sharp curve with steep banks on each side. As he started around the curve, his headlights suddenly revealed a pickup truck parked in such a way that both lanes of the highway were completely blocked.

Seeing that there was not enough space for him to drive around either end of the truck, he had just enough time to stop the car a few feet from it. He had barely got his car stopped when he saw Mike Devlin and two other men coming down the embankment.

"Where you going, Grover Danford?" he heard somebody call to him. "What's your big hurry?"

Before he could say anything, one of the men jerked open the rear door of the sedan and quickly swept the beam of a flashlight over the back seat and on the floor between the two seats. After that the door was closed with a forceful slam.

"Don't think about rushing off," Mike said as he came walking slowly up to the side of the car. "Nobody else ain't in no hurry around here at this time of night. It's nice and early. Pull your car over to the side of the road and stay around awhile."

"I don't have time for that."

"Why not?"

"I want to keep on going," Grover told him.

"Why? What for?"

"There's something I want to attend to down the road."

"What?"

"It's something important."

"Hell, you know you don't go around like this trying to sell your fancy little horses in the dark, now do you? Hell, people want to see what they're getting in the daylight, now don't they?"

When Grover remained silent, Mike kicked the side of the sedan with a hefty swing of his foot.

"Hell, it's real early yet—Grover. I'm not on the job now and I don't have to call you Mr. Danford, do I, Grover? Now go ahead and move your car off the road so you won't be blocking it for people who might come along with a good reason to have some kind of business to take care of in the nighttime—Grover."

While he was driving his car to the side of the highway, somebody moved the pickup truck out of the way. When the headlights of both the truck and the sedan were switched off, the moonlight was bright enough then for Grover to see the handle of a pistol that Mike Devlin had in his pocket and the gleam of light on the barrel of a shotgun that a tall, thin-faced man with close-cropped black hair was holding in the crook of his arm. The man with the shotgun was as much of a stranger to Grover as was the short, tubby-bellied man with the flashlight, and he decided that both of them had come from some distant community in the county.

"What's this all about, Mike?" he asked.

"You'll find out," Mike told Grover when he got out of the car. Mike's rough manner of speaking sounded more like an order than anything else. "Let's climb on up to the top of this here bank. There's a nice place up there on top where everybody can sit down and scratch his balls and not have to stand around down here on the road. Hell, somebody might come speeding around this curve in a big car and run over us and kill us dead if we stayed down here. Nobody likes to get killed, do they—Grover?"

Mike Devlin and the two strangers had been the only men within sight when Grover got out of his car.

However, there were three other men waiting at the top of the bank when he got there. By then his vision was much better in the moonlight and he knew at once who the other men were. One of them was a gasoline station owner named Nobby Johnson; another was Bundy Godowns, who was a carpenter and bricklayer and handyman; and, most surprising of all, the third person was Preacher Scoggins, a thirty-year-old bachelor minister who had recently come to Wolverton to be the pastor of the Unity Brotherhood Church.

Chapter

EIGHT

The three men Grover had recognized in the moonlight when he climbed to the top of the slippery red-clay incline were sitting on a thick ground cover of dry pine needles at the edge of a stand of full-grown trees. Nobby Johnson, still wearing his green cloth cap and greasy filling station uniform with the gasoline company's five-year merit badge, was leaning back against a pine tree and calmly smoking his pipe just as if he had been sitting on the bank of a creek and patiently waiting for a bite on his fishline. Bundy Godowns and Preacher Scoggins were sitting cross-legged not far from Nobby with their heads close together and whispering confidentially.

Not a word was said to Grover as he waited in the clearing while Mike Devlin and the other two men were climbing up the steep bank behind him.

An automobile, its headlights flashing in the night, went speeding around the curve below, and he wondered how Mike and the other men knew he was coming when he did and were prepared to roadblock him with the truck. He decided that somebody—probably a farmer living on the back road—had seen him leaving home and had telephoned the information to whoever was waiting for the call.

There was a mild southerly breeze faintly rustling the pine boughs overhead and the only other sound to be heard after the speeding automobile had gone down the highway toward Tupelo was the grunting of Mike Devlin and the two men as they got to the clearing. After they had squatted near Nobby and the others, and as he stood there facing all six of them, Grover felt as if he were on trial before a prejudiced judge and jury that had already decided in advance among themselves to order death for both Jeff and himself.

As he thought of Jeff being helpless in the trunk of the sedan, he blamed himself and Jim Whittaker for failing to think of a safer method of getting the boy away from Wolverton.

"Grover, I reckon you know everybody here except for Ed and Howie," Bundy Godowns, lazily and unhurriedly, said presently in a friendly manner, as if all seven of them had just happened to meet on Union Street in Wolverton. "There's always bound to be somebody in a crowd like this who's a stranger to somebody else, ain't there? A man can't expect to know everybody in the whole country to start with, can he?"

Bundy, a round-faced stocky man about forty years old with bristly yellowish hair, was wearing his usual grimy gray work shirt and pants. His broad smile gave him the appearance of being friendly-mannered and congenial, but he was known for becoming quickly angered and quarrelsome when something displeased him. He had several children and his oldest son was a guard on the high school basketball team. Bundy was always present and loudly rooting at every game played in Wolverton and several times had left his seat and knocked down the referee when he was displeased with a ruling against the home team. And only the year before on a construction job he got into an argument and shot a Negro helper to death, but he claimed self-defense and was never arrested or tried in court for the killing.

"Ain't I right about that what I said, Grover?" he called out loudly.

Grover nodded.

"Well, that being the case, Grover, I reckon you want to know all about Ed and Howie so they won't keep on being strangers to you. They know all about you and how you raise those little sawed-off horses and it's only fair for you to get acquainted with them."

Grover, increasingly worried about Jeff and hoping to get the ordeal over with as soon as possible, had nodded immediately to Bundy. However, Bundy was unhurried and he sat smiling friendlily for several moments as if taking delight in prolonging the ordeal.

"I think I'll start out and tell you about Ed Bridger first, Grover," he said presently. "That's the right thing to do, being as how he looks the oldest even if he ain't. That's Ed Bridger squatting down there in his faded old overalls and slouchy old dusty hat that some rats used to nest in before he came along and snatched it away from them. Ed won't go out and buy nothing new he can get hold of just by taking. I ain't charging he does common stealing. No, sir! Not Ed! What he does is just take his time and waits till he figures a certain thing has outlived its usefulness for somebody where it was and then he

84

comes along and picks it up and walks off with it. Ed's been one of the boys ever since I can remember. How old are you now, Ed?"

"Plenty old enough to suit my ways," he answered in a deep-down throaty voice. "Don't need to add no more to it. Got a good feeling being just like I am right now."

"You hear that, Grover?" Bundy said with his round-faced smile. "He sounds old as hell the way he talks, don't he? Now I'll tell you some more about him. Ed comes from way up Bushy Creek near the county line and grinds corn in his water mill up there for people who don't want to have to go without their cornbread to sop up their molasses with for their eating habits three times a day. That's what Ed does when he ain't too busy out in the woods cooking mash to make his corn liquor. They say the healthiest people in the whole county are raised up there where they can eat plenty of Ed Bridger's water-ground cornmeal. And his corn liquor kills off germs and tapeworms lightning fast and keeps everybody up there healthy between meals. That's why there ain't no sickly people up there. A medicine doctor would starve to death if he tried to make a living in Ed Bridger's neighborhood treating bowel troubles and female complaints. You didn't rush off and fail to bring a sample jug of your makings down here with you, did you, Ed?"

"Me and the jug both goes everywhere together," he answered with a bullfroggy hoarseness. "Wouldn't even make consent to go to jail without it. Got so I can go a heap longer time not fooling around with my old woman on her quilt than I can without my jug."

Bundy turned and pointed his finger at the lean-faced man in faded blue overalls who was wearing a wide-brimmed, sun-scorched field-straw hat with the brim pulled over his eyebrows. He had been carefully honing the blade of his pocketknife on the sole of his shoe while Bundy was talking about Ed Bridger.

"Now that's Howie Smithly there. Howie ought to be younger than old Ed is but you can't tell for sure because he always looks like he's got a crop of three-day yellow whiskers on his face. Howie could get shaved at the barbershop at closing time late on Saturday night and go home and on Sunday morning at church preaching he'd still look like he hadn't shaved for three days. If his wife was a modern woman, she wouldn't put up with all the scratching she has to take from him.

"Anyhow, Howie lives over in the Perky Peter neighborhood on the west side of the county. Grover, you've heard of Perky Peter. Howie claims he was the one who named that neighborhood over there what it is because that's the way he used to feel a long time back when he woke up in the sunny spring mornings. He says certain conditions now ain't like they used to be for him at no time of the year but he don't mind that too much because it makes him feel good just to remember about it in the old days.

"Well, to get along now, Howie farms a little cotton patch or pea patch or a puny patch of something or other when he feels like it, which ain't too often, and the rest of the time he runs a little skinny-assed grocery store over there where he sells canned salmon and salt pork and cheats hell out of all the blacks living for miles around Perky Peter because there ain't no other store where they can buy at without having to come all the way to Wolverton. Howie says he likes to cheat niggers because that's the best way he knows how to prove how much he hates the sight of their black hides. Just like Ed Bridger, Howie's been one of the boys a long time, too. He's real faithful that way."

Howie raised his hand and waved it at Grover.

"Now I reckon you're acquainted with everybody here, Grover," Bundy said. "Sit down and make yourself feel comfortable. We ain't going nowhere for a while. We've got all the time in the world to spare and can do a lot of talking. Well, I've been doing all this talking so far and now you can tell me something. How about it, Grover?"

"What do you want to know?" he asked Bundy.

"Where'd you start out to go off to tonight? And where's that near-white nigger boy who works for you? You know who I'm talking about."

"I told you when you stopped my car that I had something to attend to down the road," Grover said as calmly as he could. "That ought to be enough to say."

"But you still ain't told about the nigger," Mike Devlin called out loudly. "That's what I want to know. Where the hell is he at? I went to Pete Lawson's house looking for him and Pete and his wife both tried to claim they didn't know nothing about where he was. That didn't satisfy me and I walked right inside and went looking all through Pete's house—in closets and under beds and all hiding places—but couldn't find him hiding nowhere in it. That made me mad as hell and I told Pete Lawson I'd skin his black hide off of him even if he was a cripple if I ever found out he was telling me a big lie saying he didn't know where Jeff Bazemore was."

"Just a minute, folks," Preacher Scoggins said in a solemn voice as he was getting to his feet. He took off his hat and placed it where he had been sitting on the pine-needle ground cover. "I'm a minister of the gospel and I hear my duty calling me. When I hear that, everything else has got to stand aside and wait awhile. My duty comes first."

Preacher Scoggins was a tall, thin, dark-haired man with heavy black eyebrows that grew low on his forehead and came together above his nose without the slightest gap to separate them. He was wearing dusty dark blue pants and a rumpled white shirt with the collar buttoned high under his chin without a necktie.

"Now listen here to me, you folks," he said gravely, walking in long strides across the clearing and then coming back to stand in front of the group. He ran his fingers through his shaggy black hair several times before pushing it away from his forehead with a quick thrust of his hand. "Folks, we need God on our side at a time like this. We want God to bless us. Folks, let's have a little prayer first."

"Amen!" somebody in the group said.

Preacher Scoggins waited, looking from one person to the next, until everybody had taken off his hat and bowed his head. Then he coughed several times and cleared his throat as if testing the clarity and volume of his voice.

"Almighty God, look down here at us in these pretty piney woods on this beautiful night," he began in a calmly even tone. There was a long pause then as he tilted back his head and gazed at the starry sky. "Almighty God, heaven's a beautiful sight up there tonight for the whole sinful world to see, but everybody knows there's no sinning up there like down here. Everybody knows what an awful sinful place it is down here, but people like us do our best to go around and put a stop to all the sinning down here we can. And that's what we're right here for now."

"You said it, Preacher!" somebody called out. "Amen!"

"Almighty God, all of us down here know we are a little bit sinful one way or other, which the Bible allows for if we repent and don't go out and do over again too often. And some people are more sinful than others, which is getting mighty close to what the Bible don't allow. That's when now and then some people go just too far and repenting ain't good enough for the sin they done. What I'm talking about is when somebody's gone and intercoursed a good white woman's sex without being her color. And people like us know we're duty-bound to get out and track down the sinner and make him sorry for doing what the Bible don't allow. Almighty God! That's exactly why we're gathered together here like this tonight to get the right thing done about it before the sinner gets away and gone!"

"That's telling 'em, Preacher Scoggins!" one of the men called out. "Keep it up, Preacher!"

First he wiped his face and forehead with the sleeve of his shirt and then, taking several short steps as he loudly cleared his throat again and again, he moved around nervously. His shirttail was coming out and he stuffed some of it back into his pants. When he was ready to continue, he first took a long deep breath.

II

"Almighty God!" Preacher Scoggins began then with a quavering shout that echoed again and again in the pine grove as though it had been relayed from tree to tree. His glance upward at the sky was brief and hurried as he raised both arms above his head and began waving his hands excitedly. "Don't let that sinful nigger boy get away from us! Help us track him down and make him suffer for what he done! Just think of that poor white woman getting intercoursed in her sex and made to have a part-colored baby. And don't forget her poor white husband who was faithfully working at his job and couldn't be there to beat him off. Oh, it's a terrible thing! But we'll take care of what needs to be done when we find him. Leave that to us. Oh, Lord! Don't fail us good people now. Help us. Open our eyes. Lead us. Show us the right way to go from here so we won't waste time. Time! Precious time! We're all ready to get up and go!"

Some of the men were already getting up from the ground and stretching their legs.

"You tell'm, Preacher!"

"Praise God!" another man shouted.

Preacher Scoggins unbuttoned his shirt collar and wiped the perspiration from his face and neck with one hand while still waving his other hand above his head. Realizing that he had moved forward until he was standing in the shadow of a pine bough, he quickly stepped backward until he was in the moonlight again.

"Almighty God!" His quavering voice then sounded as if he had finally reached the limit of his endurance. "bless us for setting out for what needs to be done! Bless all us good people! Don't let us stumble on stony ground! Don't let us fall by the wayside! Don't let the old devil mislead us down the wrong path! Almighty God! Give us the guiding light for our footsteps! Make the light shine bright! Open our eyes to the right path to take! Lead us to the sinner! Damn the sinner to hell!"

In the end, his voice was so weak that all he could do was close his eyes and bow his head in benediction.

Grover was the last to get to his feet and he stood aside while the other men were crowding around Preacher Scoggins and shaking his hand and slapping him on the back. The minister's shirttail was hanging outside his pants and his white shirt was wet with sweat. His damp shaggy black hair lay over his forehead to the top of his eyebrows and his shoulders drooped weakly from exhaustion. After so much shouting his voice was so hoarse that he could barely whisper a few words as he nodded with an appreciative smile when he heard the approving comments around him.

"You sure know how to go after that old red-eyed devil and give him hell," Nobby Johnson was saying to him. "It does my soul good to hear you give the old devil what's coming to him after putting that nigger boy up to what he done. The next time you hold a revival at your church you're going to see me right there listening to you in a front-row seat. You ain't timid about speaking out like a preacher ought to."

"Preacher Scoggins," somebody else said, "an old frog jumped down your throat while you did all that praying and what you need is a good hearty swallow from Ed Bridger's jug. That'll drown that old frog in there. Come on. We'll go down to the truck where Ed's jug's at."

Mike Devlin and Bundy were walking slowly to Grover at the edge of the clearing. He knew what they were going to demand to be told and he had been thinking all that time how he could keep them from suspecting where Jeff was. It seemed hours since he had been stopped on the highway and he wondered how much longer Jeff could endure being cramped in the trunk of the sedan without becoming desperate and making some sound that the men would hear. He remembered that when he left the stables he had been confident that he could get far enough away after no more than an hour so he could safely let Jeff get out of the trunk.

From the moment he had to stop his car to avoid running into the pickup truck, he had had the constant fear that one of the men was going to suspect that the trunk could be Jeff's hiding place and hold a gun on him and force him to unlock it. He had been thoughtful enough to take the keys from the car when he left it beside the highway and since then, when nobody was watching, he had been putting his hand into his pocket to make certain they were still there.

As Mike and Bundy came closer then, he was sure they were going to order him to open the trunk.

"Everybody hurry up and finish your pissing and let's go," somebody called out. "We got business to attend to. We're wasting too much time here now."

Bundy Godowns gave Grover a shove with his elbow and all of them went to the top of the bank and one by one slid down to the bottom and leaped over the ditch to the road. Several automobiles and trucks had already gone by while they were at the clearing and another car came speeding around the curve then. The driver did not even slow down as he went past.

"All right, Grover Danford," Mike told him. "Now's when you can start talking. You've had plenty of time to think it over and by now you know what we want to know. It won't do you no good to keep on acting like you don't know where that nigger boy's at."

"Maybe Grover don't know where he's at no more than we do," Bundy said, looking straight at Mike. "You can't make a man say what he don't know."

"Who says I can't?"

"I do."

"You fat-assed bastard, you!" Mike yelled at him angrily. "That's no way to talk! You keep that up and we'll stand around here all night and not find out nothing! Now you keep your mouth shut and I'll do the talking!"

"Goddam it, Mike Devlin, nobody named you the big-mouth boss. Who in hell do you think you are? You've got no more say-so about it than anybody else."

"You son of a bitch! You just wait till your wife gets raped by a nigger like mine did—and then don't expect me to feel sorry about it!"

"Well, I've heard it said it ain't always one-sided. And there're two kind of women in this world. I know about my wife but I don't know about yours. And if you didn't see it with your own eyes—"

Mike stepped backward, reaching for his pistol. Before he could jerk it from his hip pocket, Nobby Johnson locked his arms around Mike and Howie Smithly took the pistol away from him.

"Goddam you, Howie, give me back my gun!"

"Calm down, Mike," Howie said. "Cool yourself off. We're not getting nowhere like this. I'm not convinced that Grover Danford knows where the nigger is. But if you know where he's at, say so and let's go get him. And if you don't know now, I'm going home. I don't aim to stay around here all night and lose my sleep for nothing. I've got plenty of work to do in the daytime."

"Don't go off, Howie. I know where to find him. We need you to help. He wasn't hiding at home in Pete Lawson's house, for one thing. And he's smart enough to know it wouldn't do him no good to try to hide out in Grover Danford's stables and barns. He knows he'd be easy to find like that. But I know where to look for him. Now give me back my gun and let's go."

III

Ed Bridger had gone to the truck for his jug and a tin cup. After pouring some of the corn liquor into the cup, he took it to Preacher Scoggins. The minister, firmly shaking his head and waving both hands in protest, backed away from it.

"I wouldn't want it known that I touched a drop of what you've got there."

"Nobody'll know about it but us, Preacher, and we won't tell," Ed said, following him with the cup and holding it closer to him. "Go ahead, Preacher. It wouldn't be polite for us to take a drink and you didn't have none. And I never did like to drink in front of a man who didn't take one himself. That ain't good sociable hospitality. And that hoarse throat of yours could give you some bad trouble and you couldn't preach a fine sermon next Sunday if you don't give it a good dose of medicine to kill off all the nasty slimy germs that old frog's hatching in there and trying to make trouble for you."

Ed held the cup so close to Preacher Scoggins' nose that every time he sniffed the fumes his head jerked backward.

"Well, if it's good medicine—"

"Nobody's come up with none better so far."

He reached for the tin cup, jamming his forefinger into the handle, and took a cautious sip from it as though accustomed to testing the quality of anybody's homemade corn liquor before committing himself. After licking his lips several times and blinking with stinging tears that clouded his eyes, he quickly drank the rest of it in long gulps with his Adam's apple pumping it down his throat.

Ed refilled the cup and took his own drink before passing it along to the others. The gallon jug was almost half empty by the time it was handed to Grover.

With everybody watching him in silence, Grover knew it was no time to risk antagonizing them by refusing to drink with them. He poured a small portion into the tin cup and drank it down as quickly as he could.

"How's your throat feel now, Preacher?" Ed asked.

"Fine and dandy. Just fine and dandy."

"Give me back my gun now," Mike told Howie. "I want to get started. And I know where to go, too. I can go straight from here to that nigger's hiding place and I need my gun for that."

"Hold on here just a minute now," Bundy said, taking the pistol from Howie before Mike could get his hand on it. "I ain't satisfied. Nobody's kept after Grover Danford to tell what he knows. That's what we stopped him down here for—to find out what he knows."

"Hell, Grover don't know nothing like I do," Mike said. "And he wouldn't talk if he did. I've got it all figured out, just like I told you. That's why I know what to do about it. If Grover had been trying to get Jeff Bazemore away from here, he'd had him in that car with him, wouldn't he? But he wasn't there when Howie looked in the back seat with his flashlight, was he? Hell, no!"

"That won't prove a damn thing," Bundy said, shaking his head. "Not a goddam thing. He could still know where that boy is at. What do you know about it, Grover?"

Grover shook his head, saying not a word.

"Say something, damn it," Bundy insisted. "Is he hiding up there in one of your barns and stables? In a hayloft or somewhere?"

"I don't know anything about that."

"If you don't, who does? How about Jim Whittaker? Does Jim know where he's at?"

"That's something you'll have to ask Jim."

"What do you expect me to do—ring him up on the telephone from here? All right. While we're waiting for them to string a telephone line down here, there's something you can tell me. Why did you start going off at night somewhere in that big car of yours?"

"I've already said there's something I want to attend to down the road."

"Attend to what?"

"That doesn't matter as long as it's my own business, does it?"

"It might. It just might."

"Goddam it, Bundy, you bigmouth son of a bitch!"

Mike yelled at him. "You ain't doing a fucking thing but wasting good time, you fat-assed bastard!"

"I'm not taking much more of that." There was an angry flush on Bundy's face and he was about to point the pistol at Mike when Nobby Johnson grabbed it away just in time. "Goddam you, I'm warning you, Mike. I never did like to be cussed at before in my life and I don't like it no better now. You'd better watch your talk from now on like I'm telling you."

"Go to hell, Bundy Godowns! Nobody's scared of you!"

"You'll end up wishing you'd been scared enough to shut up—if you keep on cussing me tonight!"

Spitting on the ground between them as if daring Bundy to step over the marking, Mike turned and walked over to Grover's car and slammed his fist on top of the trunk. There was a brief moment when he stood there indecisively as he looked down at the gleam of moonlight on the shiny dark blue paint. He suddenly hit the trunk again with his fist and then turned around.

"Go on about your business, Grover Danford," he ordered. "Get going. We don't need you for what we're going to get done and you're in the way. I don't know what your business is down the road at this time of night, unless you've got a dead pony in that trunk to haul off somewhere and get rid of. That trunk looks plenty big enough to hold one of those dead little runty horses of yours. But looks like you'd dug a hole up there at your place to bury it in."

"Hell, you don't know nothing, Mike Devlin," Bundy said. "Grover's got something more important on his mind than hauling a dead pony around at this time of night. He's going off to see a woman, that's what. From what I hear, he can't make his wife stay at home and so he has to go off looking for a woman somewhere else now and then. All he has to do is keep his mouth shut about what he's heard down here tonight and I won't be telling his wife what I know about him. Now go on off about your personal business, Grover—you hear?—so we can go off and attend to ours."

Chapter

NINE

When Grover left the six men standing around the mud-splattered pickup truck and drinking again from Ed Bridger's jug, Mike and Bundy had started another loud argument. He drove slowly away southward until he had gone around the curve out of sight and was at least a mile from where he had left them. Feeling safe then when he had gone that distance and still had seen no headlights coming up behind him, he quickly put the big sedan into a burst of speed.

After going about fifteen miles down the Tupelo highway, and at times speeding as much as ninety miles an hour on straightaway stretches of the two-lane blacktop road, he slowed down the car and began looking for a secluded stopping place.

He had been watching the rear-view mirror all that time, fearful that one of the men would realize that they had let him go without looking into the trunk. However, since by then there were still no headlights of a following truck or car to be seen, he believed that he had gone far enough to make it safe for him to stop. There had not been a sound of any kind in the trunk during the whole time and, afraid that Jeff had not been able to get enough air and was unconscious, he was anxious to stop and get the trunk open.

Grover had traveled the same road many times in daylight and he thought he knew the countryside well. At that distance from Wolverton it was mostly wooded land on rolling hills and a few barbwire pastures and only an occasional farmhouse by the roadside.

Most of the people who lived there were tenants who pastured cattle or cut timber or raised corn and peas, and being in the habit of getting up at dawn to go to work, they would not stay up long after dark in the short nights of summer. Now that it was midnight, there was not a single light to be seen anywhere. The moon was becoming clouded and its light was already so faint that even the outline of rooftops on the dwellings and barns would not have been visible from the highway.

The automobile had been slowed down to only a few miles an hour when Grover came to a narrow farm lane between a fenced pasture and a pea field, and he immediately turned into it and went about a hundred yards before stopping. There had been no mailbox where the lane began at the highway and no nearby house could be seen in the glow of the headlights.

Immediately turning off the lights, Grover jerked out the keys and hurried to the rear of the car. In the darkness, and in his nervous haste, he could not find the lock to the trunk until he had got down on his knees and desperately felt for it with the tips of his fingers for what seemed like minutes and minutes.

There was not a sound from Jeff during all the time he was trying to get the trunk unlocked and the thought then in Grover's mind was that Jeff could have suffocated if he had gone to sleep with his body covering the hole that Jim Whittaker had cut in the floor of the trunk. While he was fumbling nervously in the darkness, he called Jeff several times but there was no answer. He remembered warning Jeff not to make a sound no matter who spoke to him or what happened as long as he was in the trunk and Grover still did not know if the boy would be found to be dead or alive.

Finally, his hand trembling more violently than ever, he was able to insert the key into the lock and the top of the trunk sprang open. Instantly the light inside the trunk went on and there was Jeff, his lips quivering and his eyes blinking in the unaccustomed light as he looked up at Grover.

"Good God, Jeff! Are you all right?"

Jeff's lips were still quivering as he nodded.

"Is that you, Mr. Grover?"

"Don't worry, Jeff," he said hastily. "It's me."

"It sounds like you, Mr. Grover. It's good to hear you, too."

Grover leaned forward and gripped Jeff's arm reassuringly.

"Can you see me now, Jeff?"

"I can see better all the time now. Is anybody else out there?"

"No. Nobody else. Only me."

Still blinking his eyes, Jeff wet his dry lips with the tip of his tongue as he smiled slightly.

"Where are we, Mr. Grover?"

"Somewhere in the country. And it's all right now. Don't worry about anything. We're safe enough."

"Where are all those other people I heard talking so much a while ago?"

"We got away from them. We left them behind."

"How far behind?"

"Almost back in Wolverton."

"How far away is that?"

"About fifteen miles or more."

"Will you tell me something, Mr. Grover?"

"What is it?"

"How did you keep them from looking in here for me?"

"All I could do was hope and trust to luck. And I was really worried, too, all that time. That was a dangerous situation. And it went on and on—it seemed like forever. But it ended up being lucky—that's all that matters now."

"They wanted to kill me, didn't they? I could hear a lot of what they said. I wish they wouldn't blame me about Mrs. Devlin—it was her blame—it wasn't mine. That's the truth, Mr. Grover. It was what she wanted to do. She made me stay in the weather shelter without my clothes she'd hidden and wouldn't let me go and I couldn't hit a white lady. She kept on holding me down and was so strong and heavy and then I couldn't help myself after that. You believe me, don't you, Mr. Grover?"

"I believe you, Jeff. And I understand. But let's not talk about it anymore now. We'll talk about it later. I want you to get out of there so we can get going. We still have a long way to go and it's already after midnight. You can ride up front with me the rest of the way to Tupelo. Climb out now and let's go."

Jeff, pushing himself upward on his elbow, was able to raise his head and shoulders, but he was unable to move any more after that. There was a helpless expression on his face as he looked up at Grover.

"Mr. Grover—"

"What's the matter, Jeff?"

"Mr. Grover—my legs—they won't move. There's something wrong with them—both of them. I don't know what. They feel like—like they're not there anymore. I can see them but I can't feel them at all. I'm trying, but I can't even make them move. What's wrong with them, Mr. Grover?"

"You've been cramped up like that in the trunk so long your legs are numb. That's the trouble. And we can be glad that's all that happened to you and not something worse."

He leaned over closer to Jeff.

"Put your arms around my neck and hold on tight while I lift you out of there. We'll get you fixed up in no time. I'm going to carry you to the front seat and you can sit there and go to work getting the kinks out of your legs. You'll be all right then. Now, hold on tight to me."

With the tightening of Jeff's arms around his neck, and then the warm clinging touch of their bodies when he put his own arms around Jeff and lifted him from the trunk, Grover knew he would never forget the sensation that had come over him as he held his son close to him for the first time in his life. Feeling the warmth of Jeff's breath on his neck and cheek, he tightened his arms so they would be even closer together then.

Even though he had shaken hands with Jeff many times at the stables, and had often slapped him on the back when praising him for his gentle way of handling the Shetlands, Grover knew he had been yearning all those years to be able to be alone with his son as they were now and to be able to let Jeff know of his fatherly love and affection.

As he was carrying Jeff to the front seat of the car, he was wondering whether the boy had ever suspected that he was his father or, if not, would he be too surprised to believe it when he was told.

Standing on the ground at the open door of the sedan after putting Jeff on the seat, Grover was carefully stretching and kneading his son's legs when he heard a dog begin barking not far away. There had been a painful look on Jeff's face in the beginning, but he gradually became relaxed, leaning back against the seat, and was soon smiling gratefully.

"My legs are tingling, Mr. Grover," he said presently. "I can feel it all over them now. It feels good. They feel real again."

The dog, sounding nearer this time, had begun barking again.

"That's a good sign when you can feel the tingling, Jeff. They're going to be just as good as new. You keep on working on them while I'm getting the car backed out of here to the highway. There's a house near here or somebody's dog wouldn't be barking at us. We don't want to stay here any longer and have somebody find us here."

Nothing more was said until they had backed out of the lane and gone several miles down the paved road toward Tupelo. Jeff had been bending his knees and stretching his legs all that time and by then he was no longer uncomfortable. As they both watched the winding road ahead in the bright beam of the headlights, Jeff leaned close to Grover.

"Mr. Grover—"

"What is it, Jeff?"

"I'm hungry," he said plaintively.

"I know you must be," Grover said at once. "I'm hungry, too. We didn't have a bite of supper tonight—neither of us. But I'm afraid we can't find any place to eat at this time of night till we get to Tupelo. Everybody along here has probably closed up business and gone home to sleep by now. There's not enough travel on this road to make it worthwhile to keep a restaurant open all night. Do you think you can hold out a little while longer?"

"If you can, I can, Mr. Grover."

"That's the spirit, boy. I like to hear you talk like that. It proves something."

"Do you like certain things to eat, Mr. Grover?"

"I sure do."

"Does your wife cook everything for you that you like to eat?"

"Well, it's like this, Jeff. Annie and Della do all that. They know what I like to eat and they have it for me."

"Then what is there for your wife to do?"

"She has to have a lot of medical treatments. That takes up most of her time."

"That must keep her very busy, because I never see her often."

Grover nodded. "Neither do I."

They were passing through a cluster of several small houses and a couple of roadside grocery stores. There were no streetlights in the settlement and every building was dark. As they got to the open country again, the highway curved downward to marshy bottomland and a thick growth of willows on each side of a creek.

After crossing the narrow bridge over the stream, the highway went straight ahead over a wooded ridge. There had been a few advertising signs along the road for the past several miles and now they began appearing in the bright glow of the headlights more frequently. Some old and faded, some new and freshly painted, most of the signs were close enough to the highway to be easily seen at night. Occasionally Jeff read aloud the wording of a sign as they were passing it.

Clabber Girl
Blanchard Bros. Family Clothing Store

No-Doze
Morrison Funeral Home
Fill Up At Hank Upps
Bring a Friend—Paradise Motel—$5 for Couples
Jesus Saves
Eat at Fred's Place
Dale's Farm & Home Hardware
Take Dr. Jimson's Tonic for Stomach Troubles
Texaco Ahead
Morning Joy Flour for Better Biscuits
Bee Line Truck Stop
Vote for J. A. (Jake) Hammond for Sheriff
Pappy's Root Beer
Elite Cafe
See Hankin's for Shoes First
Royal Crown Cola
Mrs. Bonner's Home Made Pies & Cakes

Jeff began stretching his legs again and moving around nervously on his side of the seat. The roadside signs were as plentiful as ever but he had stopped reading them aloud.

Grover could see Jeff looking at him questioningly.

"What is it, Jeff?" he asked.

"Mr. Grover—a little while ago—you said you liked to hear me talk a certain way. You remember that?"

"That's right, Jeff. I remember. Why?"

"You said it proves something. What did you mean by that? What does it prove?"

"Have you been thinking about that all this time?"

He nodded. "I keep on wondering about it."

They were going around a sharp curve then and Grover waited until they had passed it and were on straight roadway again. The car had been slowed down for the curve and he was still driving at a slower speed.

"I'll tell you exactly what I meant, Jeff," he said then. "It proves you take after me."

Jeff, silent and thoughtful, was staring straight ahead.

"Does that mean anything to you, Jeff?"

Jeff was slowly shaking his head.

"You're my son. I'm your father. After all this time—didn't you know that by now?"

He smiled slightly. "You're joking, Mr. Grover."

"No, Jeff. I'm not joking. And you should be calling me Dad or Papa, or something like that—not Mr. Grover. But you can't do that. It wouldn't be a good thing to do—the way things are. That's the way it happens to be. Anyway, this is a secret between us and the only way to keep the secret is for you to keep on calling me by my name the way you've been doing. Will you promise me that, Jeff?"

Jeff was moving nervously on his side of the seat.

"Mr. Grover—I promise what you said—but I just can't believe it somehow."

"Wouldn't you like to believe it?"

"Well, yes, but—"

"But what?"

"Well, how could you be that? Mama and Papa Lawson say I'm an orphan. You're white, too. I'm not white like you."

"Jeff, even an orphan has to have had a father of some color to begin with—you know that. And you can think you're an orphan, just as Mary and Pete Lawson told you, but that doesn't mean you didn't have a mother—and that I can't be your father. And I am. That's the truth, Jeff. I ought to know. And I'm glad I can tell you now. I've wanted to for a long time. I didn't know how to go about telling you before—but tonight—after getting you away from those men—I didn't want to wait any longer. And now's the time. And now you know."

He glanced at Jeff.

"What do you think about it now—son?"

II

Not a single car or truck had overtaken them since they had left the farm lane and they had not even met one until the bright blinding beam of headlights suddenly appeared as they reached the crest of a hill, and then just as quickly went past and disappeared behind them in the night.

After going down the hill and crossing another lowland creek where tall green willows hung over the water in a drooping canopy, the roadside began sparkling with dew on the grass and weeds that covered ditches and banks. At the top of the next grade, the road straightened out as it went across a broad flatland of farms and fenced pastures.

Jeff sat there in silence as he stared straight ahead. He was biting his lips from time to time and squirming restlessly on the seat. They were still far from Tupelo but the roadside advertising signs and billboards were already becoming more numerous. Some of the older tin and wooden signs were either rusty or faded and barely visible while many of the newer ones were large and brightly lettered in fancy designs.

Use Red Ball Chix Feed
St. Joseph Aspirin
First Time—Next Time—Paradise Motel—$5 for Couples
S. J. McMasters Chevrolet Sales & Service
Visit Colossal Cave
Marianne's Beauty Shoppe
Elite Cafe
Don't Go Wrong—Go to Long—for Cut-Rate Drugs
Drink Coca-Cola
Use Samson Chain Saws for Best Results
Little Red Rooster Nite Club
Trust a Country Boy for Good Used Cars—Leroy Country
Hav-A-Tampa Cigars
King Edward Cigars
Back-Home-Style Fried Chicken—The Chicken Shack
Your Best Buy—Deep South Overalls & Coveralls
Re-Elect Gilbert T. (Dusty) Rhodes for Sheriff
Try Country Life Snuff Today
Your Neighbor Has a Rutger—Why Don't You?
Jesus Christ Died for You—Stay Alive—Slow Down
See Bo Bowman for Insurance
Don't Forget—Take Home Pride-of-the-Country Grits
Honeymoon Sweets—Paradise Motel—$5 for Couples
Why Worry?—See Friendly Loan Company Today

Grover had glanced cautiously at Jeff several times, wondering what thoughts were running through his mind and how long it would take him to become convinced that he was his father. Presently, Jeff turned toward him and momentarily they were looking directly at each other.

"Well, Jeff," Grover said after that, smiling encouragingly, "what do you think about it now?"

Jeff was slow to answer.

"Mr. Grover—if you say that's the way it was—"

"It's the way it was, Jeff."

There was another long moment of silence.

"And you really knew my mother—like that?"

"Yes. Like that."

"My mother was colored and you are white—"

"That's the way it was."

He spoke up quickly. "But you and her—"

They glanced at each other again.

"Go ahead and say it," Grover urged.

"My mother and you—you and her—you didn't—you never got married?"

Grover was shaking his head. "Jeff, you know enough to know it couldn't be done here. It's never been allowed in this part of the country. Maybe someday. But it certainly wasn't permitted then. I don't know how soon it could change. Maybe ten years—twenty—thirty. Or maybe next year. But that will never make any difference now—I mean, about what's already happened—what happened long ago—soon after you were born. And you're here now—that's what matters."

"About me—I want to know—was it because my mother wanted me to be born?"

"That's something you can bet on all your life, Jeff," he said at once. There was a long pause after that until he spoke again. "We were in love—that's the reason. Someday you'll know yourself what it's like to be in love and what it can mean to two people—a man and a woman. Anyway, I loved her and she loved me. And don't you ever think otherwise about it. It was nothing like what sometimes happens when a white man—well, I mean when a man forces a woman to do what he wants—or if she can force him—"

Suddenly realizing the implication of what he had said, he glanced at Jeff. In the dim reflection from the headlights, he had seen the tensely worried expression on Jeff's face.

"It was different with your mother and me," he said hastily. "That's what I mean. It was just as if we'd been the same color. And I'll tell you something else. If your mother and I could've been married—if the law hadn't kept us from getting married because of our different color—your name now would be Jeff Danford and not Jeff Bazemore. But since it couldn't be Danford, I want you to be proud of having the same name your mother had. Bazemore. Kathlee . . . Kathlee . . . Bazemore. Always be proud of it, Jeff."

He turned to Grover, nodding and smiling.

"That's a pretty name . . . Kathlee . . . Kathlee."

"It sure is, Jeff. To me it'll always be the prettiest name there is. It's as pretty as your mother was."

"Was she very pretty, Mr. Grover?"

Grover nodded. "Yes. Very much so."

"I don't remember—I don't even know what she looked like—I never knew."

"Of course not. You were only a baby when she died."

"Why did she die?"

"Didn't Mary or Pete ever tell you?"

"All they said was that my mother died soon after I was born. Why did she?"

With his gaze fixed on the road ahead, Grover took a long deep breath before answering. Even though he disliked talking about it, he realized that Jeff was old enough now to know the truth about what had happened to his mother.

"Somebody killed her—"

"How?"

"With a gun."

"A white man?"

"No."

"A colored man! Why did he do that?"

There was a tightening of his lips and his voice was sharp and angry in tone.

"Why, Mr. Grover? Tell me."

"He wanted her to go back to Memphis to live—that was the reason." He was speaking slowly, his voice subdued, as he recalled what had happened so long ago in the past. "She wouldn't go—she didn't want to. Your mother and I loved each other so much that she wanted to stay in Wolverton even if we couldn't be married then. What we were planning to do later—if she hadn't been murdered—was to go away where we could get married. We knew we couldn't come back here to live after that and I was going to sell the farm and begin raising ponies somewhere else. A group of horsemen from Kentucky made me a good offer and then—then that happened to her. That's when I took it off the market and decided to keep it."

The automobile had been slowed down until they were going only a few miles an hour.

"Why is my name Jeff, Mr. Grover? Who named me?"

"Your mother and I decided on that together. There was no particular reason. You were not named for anybody we knew. It was just because we talked about it and liked it better than any other name for you. Do you like it?"

"Sure. I like it fine. I'm glad you and my mother gave it to me. I wouldn't want to be named anything else."

"What you don't have, though, is a middle name, Jeff. Do you think you can go through life without an initial in the middle?"

"Do you have a middle name, Mr. Grover?"

"No."

"Then I don't need one. I want to be like you."

Grover speeded up the big sedan then and they rode in silence for several miles.

The moon was still clouded and, although there were more and more mailboxes along the roadside, farmhouses were still dark and unseen in the night. The headlights of a fast-moving automobile suddenly came up behind them and, with a blasting of the horn, went past with such speed that it was soon out of sight.

By then they were not far from Tupelo, though still not close enough to see the lights of the city, and the roadside signs and billboards were becoming more elaborate in design and vivid in color. In a sleepy voice, Jeff was reading some of the wording aloud.

It's Time to Give Your Wife a Treat—Take Her to Ching Ho's to Eat

We Make Fast Loans and Slow Collections—Confidential Loan Company

Holsum Bread

We Are Open All Day, Too—Paradise Motel—$5 for Couples

All Mother Dogs & Cats Are Permitted to Litter Free—Everybody Else $100 Fine

When You Think of Diamonds—Think of Crescent Jewelers

Don't Go Back Home Hungry—Come to the Elite Cafe

Dr. Pepper

Make Sure to Be Here for the Second Coming of Jesus Christ—Stay Alive—Slow Down

If You Ain't Got a Rutger—You Just Ain't Living

There's a Lot to Do in Biloxi

You Won't Lose Time If You Come to Hardee's for Clock & Watch Repairs

Give Yourself a Treat—Drink Kola Kola

Don't Wish You Had—Be Glad You Did—Paradise Motel—$5 for Couples

With the first pale streak of dawn over the eastern horizon, Jeff was slumping wearily against the seat. In a few moments after he had stopped reading the advertising signs he was sound asleep with his head resting against Grover's shoulder.

So that the motion of steering the car would not disturb Jeff and keep him from sleeping for a little while, Grover dropped his right hand from the steering wheel and drove more slowly with his other hand.

He sat there then feeling the slight swaying movement of Jeff's head on his shoulder and glanced from time to time at the boy's pale tan face and tousled brown hair. Thinking of all the years when he was unable to be close to his son as he was now, and wondering what was going to happen in the future, his vision became blurred just as if he had driven into a bank of dense fog.

Grover was almost completely blinded when he finally wiped his eyes with a swift motion of his one free hand in order to be able to see where he was going.

Even though Grover had tried to be careful with the motion of his hand and arm, Jeff moved his head restlessly in his sleep and began talking in a pleading voice.

"I don't want to go off and stay with anybody else. I want to stay with you. Please don't leave me—take me back with you . . . please . . . please. . . ."

Chapter

TEN

In the cool, dewy dampness of the summer morning with the sun still far below rooftop level, the only people to be seen that early on the outlying avenues of the city were Negro maids in their white uniforms on the way to prepare breakfast in the costly new brick houses and older paint-cracked wooden mansions.

The downtown streets were deserted and quiet.

It was too early for anybody to be going to work in an office and none of the stores had been opened for the day's business. However, looking as though they were routinely performing an accustomed daily morning chore, flocks of energetic sparrows were busily pecking at the litter in the gutters as they went in hops and flutters from block to block along the street.

Coming from somewhere in the distance, the rumbling noise of a heavy truck on one of the main highways occasionally filled the streets with roaring waves of sound until the rumble gradually vanished beyond hearing. Now and then there was a monotonous chugging of a diesel switch engine in the railroad freight yard not far away.

The only other sound to be heard that early in the morning was the methodical click-click of the signal switches as the traffic lights at the street corners were constantly changing from red to green and back to red again.

There was only one automobile parked on the street. It was a police patrol car in which two white-shirted city policemen were lolling comfortably with heads resting on the back of the seat while waiting to turn on the loud, shrill-toned siren and go charging after the first motorist of the day who failed to wait for the green light.

Driving carefully ever since reaching the city boundary, going slower than the warning of the posted speed limit and waiting patiently at the traffic lights, Grover had passed the patrol car and gone several blocks farther down the street before finding a restaurant that was open at that time of morning.

106

Jeff had been curled up in the corner of the seat for the past several miles and he was still sound asleep when Grover stopped at the brightly lighted Elite Cafe to go inside to get something he could bring to the car for them to eat. He knew it would make no difference whether or not there was a white-only notice on the restaurant door. He had seen Negroes ignored and unserved at lunch counters many times, or forcibly ejected, and he knew some method could be used to keep Jeff from being served at table or counter.

When Grover came back to the car, he had coffee and milk in paper cups and doughnuts and half a dozen fried-egg-and-ham sandwiches in a large brown paper bag. Immediately driving away from the parking lot of the Elite Cafe, he went several blocks and then turned down a tree-lined residential street and stopped in front of a vacant lot.

After Grover had shaken him awake, Jeff sat up and rubbed his eyes and looked around at the unfamiliar surroundings. There were dwellings of various sizes and designs on both sides of the street. A few of the houses were two or three stories in height, others were white-painted bungalows with screen porches, and all of them were set back from the street on deep lots and had wide oak-shaded lawns.

Both of them were eating hungrily when the police patrol car came to a stop beside the sedan.

One of the policemen immediately called to Grover.

"You having some kind of car trouble?"

Grover shook his head. "No trouble."

"What you doing here then?"

"Eating."

"Where you from?"

"Wolverton."

"That's pretty far away to come here to eat."

Grover nodded.

"What else did you come here for?"

"I came on business."

"How long do you figure on staying in town?"

"I don't know yet—but probably not long."

The policeman turned and said something to the driver seated beside him. A few moments later he got out of the patrol car as the driver turned on the two-way radio and began talking to somebody at the police station.

"What's that colored boy doing sitting in there on the front seat eating with a white man like you?" he said, looking through the window at Jeff. "I don't know what

107

it's like where you come from, but we're not much used to something like that down here."

At a time like that, Grover could not keep from wishing that Jeff could be miraculously transformed into a boy without his racial coloring. However, no matter how disturbed he felt at such a time, he invariably began thinking of Jeff's mother and that was when he realized that after all those years his son would be like a stranger in appearance and personality if he were different in any manner.

"Didn't you hear what I said?" the policeman asked impatiently.

"It's all right," Grover told him. "We're going now."

"Not so fast, you. I'll tell you when to go. Let me see your driver's license."

After the license had been handed to him, he made a close study of it and then looked straight at Grover.

"Are you one of the civil rights people?"

Grover shook his head. "No. I'm a stockman. I raise Shetland ponies."

"And your name is Grover Danford, huh?"

"That's right."

"What's that colored boy's name?"

"Jeff Bazemore."

"Then he's no kin to you then, huh? For a minute there I thought you and him looked a little bit alike."

Without another word, he took the license to the patrol car and handed it to the driver, who read Grover's name and address aloud into the radiophone.

"We don't want him," the driver called out a few minutes later. "Let him go."

"O.K., you," the policeman said as he handed back the license. "But this's no place to stop and eat. You hear? You ought've done that back at the Elite Cafe where you went in a little while ago—and then let that colored boy eat at one of their own places. People who live on this street are mighty particular and they won't like what you're doing here. You might throw some scraps on their nice lawn grass and make it look messy. That wouldn't be sanitary, neither, would it? You'd better move along now and go somewhere else to do your eating out of that brown paper bag."

The patrol car roared away, and at the next corner, with tires screeching, it turned and went out of sight down a side street. As Grover drove toward the Negro section of town, careful not to go any faster than the speed limit, he watched the rear-view mirror, but the patrol car was not seen following them then.

II

The first man Grover stopped to speak to when they got to the other part of town said he did not know anybody named Bazemore and had never even heard the name before. He walked away hurriedly as if fearful of being seen talking to a strange white man who was driving a large automobile with a light-skinned colored boy riding beside him instead of sitting on the back seat of the car.

The sun was rising over the treetops then and people were leaving the small unpainted houses and going off to their jobs for the day. At the next corner there was a small grocery and meat store where two elderly Negro men were sitting on a bench under the overhanging tin roof.

Grover stopped the car in front of the store and got out to speak to the men.

"Good morning," he said to them.

"Morning," each one said right away. "Morning."

"Looks like it's starting out to be a nice day for this time of summer. I don't see any rain clouds moving in, but maybe the crops need a good soaking rain now."

"What you coming here talking about like that for, white folks?" the thin-faced black man said suspiciously. "What do you need rain for?"

"I raise ponies and I need good pasturing for them. And a good hay crop, too."

"You do? That's what you raise? Well, then you ought to be just like a lot of other country people—depending on how favorable the weather's going to be."

"That's right," Grover agreed. "Everybody with crops and stock is in the same fix when it comes to weather."

He smiled at Grover then, no longer gruff and scowling. "I didn't know what to make of you when you walked up here just now. I suspicioned you to be one of the city people. They don't care nothing about what happens to folks out there on the land."

"They sure could use a good rain out there on the crops about now," spoke up the stout Negro who was wearing patched overalls that had been pot-boiled so many times that only a faint streaking of blue coloring remained. By that time, instead of being suspicious of the motives of a white stranger, he was genial and friendly in manner as though he had known Grover all his life and could be trustful. "I've had no crops myself for it to rain on since I moved to town but I know some folks out there who need helping rain after this long hot spell we've been having. It's going to be mighty hard on them if it don't hurry up and rain good soon."

"How are people getting along in town these days after moving here from the country?" Grover asked.

The two men on the bench glanced at each other, both of them shaking their heads and chuckling.

"I'll tell you about that, boss." The lanky stoop-shouldered man with the thin face pushed the brim of his hat high on his forehead and nodded to Grover. "There's only one difference about being here in town. And that's all the time seeing a heap more of us in the same fix right here close together in a bunch instead of the same people being spread out far apart in the country where you can't see them all at once. Otherwise, there ain't no difference where a colored man lives to be hungry and ragged."

"Ain't that the truth!" spoke up the stout man sitting beside him. "You can't say that too many times!"

"But the young people will be better off," Grover said. "They'll get a good education and better pay and better living."

"Maybe so—if it all don't take too long to come about. It's already passed us old folks by—and it'd better hurry up for the young folks. The young get mighty restless fast these days and it'll take a lot better living for the colored to calm them down. They want something better right now and not some other time. I'm used to the old ways and won't make no trouble. But that ain't so with the young folks I see around here and listen to their talk. They can talk so wild it makes the old-time folks want to go off and hide somewhere."

Grover had been walking back and forth in front of the two men on the bench. The door of the grocery and meat store was open but there had been no customers coming or going since he got there.

"If you're getting ready to leave now," the stout Negro said, "there's just one thing I'm curious about you. What did you stop here to talk to us for?"

"You know most of the people who live in this part of town, don't you?"

"If I don't know them, they'd know about me," said the other man, chuckling to himself. "I sure been living around here long enough for it to be one way or the other. Who you looking for, boss? What's his name?"

"Do you know somebody named Bazemore?"

"There's only one Bazemore I know of. That's old Luther. But he's got a wife, too. She's Ethel. There used to be a few young Bazemores but they moved somewhere else a long time ago. You must be talking about old Luther. I see him once in a while. Maybe that's who you want to know about."

"Where does he live?"

The two men glanced at each other.

"What do you want to see Luther Bazemore about, boss?" the tall straw-hatted man then asked in a cautious manner. "If you're the law going after old Luther for something he ain't done—"

"No, no." Grover spoke up quickly. "It's nothing like that. Don't worry. It's personal business—it's about his family. That's all I want to see him about."

"But that's what I told you when you started asking about him. Luther's children don't live here no more. They're scattered everywhere all over the country except here in Tupelo. I don't know exactly how many but there was a big heap of them."

"That won't matter. All I want is to talk to him."

"Did you come a long way to see him?"

"All the way from Wolverton."

"That is a long way off."

While Grover was walking back and forth again on the sidewalk in front of the store he could see from the corner of his eyes that the two men were whispering and still trying to decide if they felt it was safe to trust a strange white man.

"Who's that light-skin colored boy sitting out there in your big automobile?" he was asked presently. "I never saw him before. He looks like he don't live around here. Did you bring him here with you?"

"Yes. I'm taking him to see the Bazemores."

"But he wouldn't be kin to them, would he?"

Grover nodded. "He's kin."

"Well, I didn't know a black man like Luther Bazemore had any kinfolks with that mixed-in white color." He was shaking his head as he spoke. "But I've seen enough over the years now to know it can happen to anybody."

He stood up then and pointed down the street.

"You go down that way exactly two blocks from right here and you'll come to a little old flat-roof plank-sided church on the corner with no steeple on it. Then you take the right-hand way around the side of that church and go down the dirt street for two more blocks past a lot of shacky houses and then you'll come to a plank house painted a sort of brown color and with a wood-stick fence around it and a front porch that's all screened in. That's where Luther Bazemore lives and you'll find him there if he ain't off doing a little carpentry work somewhere today. He sort of takes it easy these days at his age and can't do too much work."

"Thanks for telling me how to find him," Grover said as he started toward his car. "I appreciate it a lot."

"You're welcome, boss," said the stout Negro in a way of speaking that sounded unmistakably doubtful and apprehensive. "But, please, boss, don't do old Luther no harm. He's a good hard-working man and ain't never been in trouble with the law that I know of."

"Don't worry about that," Grover called back. "This has nothing to do with the law. It's all personal."

"Thank you, boss," the tall Negro said, smiling at ease as he went back to his seat on the bench. "I sure do thank you."

As Grover drove down the street from one block to the next the sun was shining with a harsh brightness on the dilapidated and unpainted shanty-small dwellings that were crowded a few feet apart. Most of the houses had been built with doorsteps fronting on the unpaved sidewalk and did not have enough space for a front yard. There were a few, though, that had small yards with carefully tended rose bushes and jonquil beds. Elsewhere in the neighborhood there was only an occasional tree or hedge to be seen.

After turning the corner at the church, Grover drove slowly down the bumpy mud-holed dirt street, carefully steering around groups of young children playing in the mud with sticks and planks and a few wobbly-wheeled tricycles.

Standing in front of a vacant house with broken windows there were several boys of high school age who turned and watched the large dark blue sedan with sullen stares. When one of the boys picked up a handful of mud and made an exaggerated gesture of throwing it at the car and another boy took aim with an imaginary rifle, Grover wondered if he had done the right thing to bring Jeff there to stay all summer. Glancing at Jeff, he could see that the boy's face was rigid with a tight-lipped expression of unhappiness.

Nothing had been said while they were driving down the street and dodging the small children playing in the puddles. After seeing the look on Jeff's face, Grover knew that it would be better to remain silent when there was little hope of being able to say anything that would make him pleased about living in that neighborhood with his grandparents for almost three months.

III

Judging by what he had already seen since leaving the two men in front of the grocery and meat store, Grover had expected the Bazemore house to be similar to the others in the neighborhood and he was surprised to find how much better cared for it was when he stopped the car in front of it. Even though it was old and had streaks of rust on the tin roofing, the house was the largest on the street and had been built on a substantial brick foundation. Also, a neatly trimmed lawn covered the front yard and flowers grew abundantly along the edge of the screened porch and around the sides of the building. Rising above the roof could be seen the tops of several tupelo gum trees at the rear of the house.

"I want you to wait here while I go in and talk to your grandparents first," he told Jeff as he was getting out of the car. "I think that's the best thing to do."

The same tight-lipped expression remained on the boy's face and he nodded without a word as Grover left and walked toward the house. When he reached the gate, Grover looked back and saw Jeff slumping dejectedly on the seat with his chin resting on his chest. He hesitated before opening the gate, wondering at the last moment if he should go through with what he had planned but, then recalling the threats that had been made by the six men the night before, he quickly opened it and went up the path to the porch.

Grover knocked loudly on the wooden frame of the porch's screen door. There was no immediate answer. Instead of knocking again, he pressed his face against the screen and that was when he saw somebody sitting in a rocking chair on the porch. The large, stocky Negro with coal-black skin and close-cropped gray hair appeared to be about sixty-five years old. He was wearing light gray carpenter's overalls and work-scuffed tan brogans. On the floor beside the chair was a wide-brimmed, sawdust-flecked dark felt hat.

"Are you Luther Bazemore?" Grover asked.

"That's me. What do you want?"

The rocking chair squeaked faintly as it moved slowly back and forth.

"I'd like to come inside and talk to you about something."

"Talk about what?"

"I'll explain it if you'll let me in."

"Go on away from here. I ain't buying nothing."

"I'm not selling anything."

"Then who are you and what are you coming here to talk to me about?"

"That's what I want to tell you if you let me come inside."

"That won't trick me to unlock no door."

When Grover tried to open the screen door himself, he found that it was latched securely on the inside. He rapped on it then until he felt the bruising of his knuckles.

"My name is Grover Danford. I live in Wolverton. I'd like to come in and talk to you about your grandson."

"What grandson?" Luther demanded in a loud, gruff tone of annoyance. There was a faster squeaking of the rocking chair. "Grandson! I've got more of them scattered around the country than I'll ever know the names of or the looks of even if I wanted to. Who you talking about, anyhow?"

Luther remained seated in the chair, giving no indication that he intended to unlock the door and let Grover come inside.

"This is Kathlee's son I'm talking about."

The motion of the rocking chair came to a sudden stop and Luther sat up erectly.

"Kathlee! Go away from here! She's dead! She's been dead fifteen years or more. I don't know nothing about her and don't never want to. And if she had a kid while she was alive, I don't want to know nothing about that, neither. I told her to go away and stay away and never come back here. It don't make no difference to me how many kids she had. I'm black and proud of it and she was half-whitey and that proves she was no kin to me. My old woman claimed it wasn't her fault and couldn't help it when a whitey man done it but that makes no difference. I ain't got no half-whitey kin and don't want none around me. But what's a white man like you got to do with this, anyhow? What business is it of yours?"

"Kathlee's boy has worked for me for many years—he's seventeen years old now. I've got a Shetland pony farm up at Wolverton and he helps with the training. I take an interest in him—well, because his mother's dead and—"

"Why don't his own daddy do what you said instead of you? Sounds to me like his daddy was a whitey, the way you talk. That'd be just like Kathlee. She always acted

114

like she thought she was too good to be an ordinary nigger and didn't want nothing to do with blacks. I ain't so sure you don't know more about it than you're telling. Where's the boy at you're talking about?"

"He's sitting out there in the car. I'd like to bring him in here and talk to you about him."

Luther leaned back and began rocking again.

"Talk about him for what?"

"I'd like to arrrange for him to board here with you for the rest of summer—he'll be going away to school after that. And you'll be paid for his room and board—whatever amount you say you want. There won't be any argument about money. And he can help out with any kind of work you want him to do, too. You're his grandfather and—"

"I told you once already I ain't claiming kin with him or nobody like him. That Kathlee wasn't no kin to me and no kids she had won't be, neither. What made you go and bring him here for, anyhow?"

"Well, there's been some trouble in Wolverton and it's not safe for him to be there right now. This is far enough away so—"

"What kind of trouble was he in?"

"There was a woman up there—a white woman—"

"Uh-huh! That's all I need to know about it. And I could've guessed it the first time if I'd put myself to it. I don't want nothing to do with no whitey-nigger who fools around and gets in trouble over white women. He can't come here to stay no more than I'd let his whitey-nigger mother stay around no longer than she did—and I ran her off as early as I could. You get him away from here—clear out of town. I don't want nobody in this town seeing a white-nigger hanging around my house. I'm a black man and I stay proud of it and don't want nothing to do with the other kind. Go on, now. Take him away from here like I said and don't never bring him back here again."

A large, fleshy, gray-haired woman who had been standing in the doorway of the house for the past several minutes came out on the porch. Grover could not see her face distinctly through the screening while she was wiping her eyes and cheeks with the sleeve of her dress.

"Luther," she pleaded tearfully, "Luther, let him stay here. Will you, Luther? I listened to all about it. He's Kathlee's boy. She wrote me a letter all about him right after he was born—the last letter she ever wrote me just before she died. She was so proud of him. I'll take care of

115

him, Luther. I'll see to it that he never bothers you none at all. I want to take care of him for Kathlee's sake. Please, Luther—won't you say you'll let him—for just a little while—can't he stay so I can take care of him?"

"Hell, no! He ain't coming in my house. You might as well shut up about that. And keep your mouth shut about her, too. I don't want to hear nothing more about him or her."

She came across the porch and pressed her face against the screening as she looked at Jeff sitting in the car.

"What's his name?" she asked Grover.

"Jeff. Jeff Bazemore."

"Jeff," she repeated softly. "Jeff—Kathlee's boy. He hadn't even been named when she wrote me about him being born. Then she died so soon—"

She was sobbing as she leaned closer and tried to see Jeff more clearly, and her tears made little windowpanes in the screening.

"Kathlee's boy—her son—I can't see him enough! I want to go out there and see what he looks like! I want to touch him—Kathlee's boy!"

"No, you don't, Ethel!" Luther ordered roughly. He got up from the rocking chair and pushed her backward across the porch to keep her from opening the screen door. "You do what I say! You ain't going nowhere near him!"

"But Luther," she begged, "he's my grandson—can't I just go and look at him only once? I want to know what he looks like—just once, Luther. Can't I, Luther?"

"Goddam it, Ethel, you shut up about that. You know he ain't no kin to me."

"Mister, where're you going to take him from here?" Jeff's grandmother called frantically from the doorway. "Please, mister, tell me that. Will he be somewhere where I can go see him sometime?"

"I don't know," Grover told her. "If he can't stay here, I'll have to take him to Memphis and find a place he can stay."

"O Lordy! O Lordy! That's so far off and I want to see him before I die! Poor Kathlee is dead and gone and I want to see her boy before I'm dead and gone!"

"I told you to shut your mouth, Ethel!" Luther yelled at her. "I don't want to hear no more of that bawling!"

Luther came to the screen door.

"Go on away from here now with that boy," he told

Grover. "Take him off somewhere—I don't care where—
and don't never bring him back to my house again."

Grover turned away and walked down the path from
the house. By the time he had reached the gate, he realized how glad he was that he was not going to leave
Jeff to stay in the same house with Luther Bazemore. And
when he got to the car, he was smiling as he thought
about how pleased Jeff was going to be when he was told
that he would not have to stay there.

Chapter

ELEVEN

Grover got into the car and slammed the door shut without a word spoken. Jeff was looking at him questioningly but Grover wanted to wait until they had driven away from Luther Bazemore's house before explaining what had happened.

As Grover was starting the engine, Jeff's face suddenly brightened as he realized that they were leaving and that he would not have to stay there after all. With all glumness gone, he smiled for the first time that morning.

Grover, pleased and elated himself, reached over and excitedly slapped the boy on the leg. It did him good to know that he was taking Jeff away even though he realized that it would not be easy and might require a lot of time and patience to find a safe and suitable boarding place for him in Memphis or anywhere else.

They had gone only a short distance down the block when the police patrol car, suddenly coming up behind them, appeared then alongside, and one of the policemen was motioning for Grover to stop. They were the same two white-shirted men seen earlier that morning in the other part of town and evidently they had followed and had been waiting around the corner where they were able to watch him while he was at the Bazemore house.

The policeman who had motioned for Grover to stop was a burly young man, about twenty-seven or twenty-eight years old, and he was at least six feet tall and more than two hundred pounds in weight. Grover had not been aware of it earlier in the shadowy morning light, but in the bright midday sunshine he noticed that the policeman's broad, stern-looking face was pallid and that his cold gray eyes had a fixed stare that was intimidating and threatening.

"You've been driving around town all morning," he said to Grover with an accusing harshness, as if that were a violation of a city ordinance. "You said you wouldn't be staying here long, but we keep on seeing you all around town. It's getting tiresome—keeping a watch on you. How

118

much longer do you think you're going to stay here? We've got other things to do. Now, what about it?"

"I'm leaving now." Grover spoke abruptly, putting the car into gear and starting to drive away. "That ought to take care of it for you—then you can get back on the job and quit following me around."

The driver of the patrol car immediately crowded the sedan to the side of the street with a bumping of fenders.

"Not so fast, you," the burly policeman ordered roughly. "I don't like that kind of talk and I'll tell you when to go. You wait till I get through with you. Now, I want to know something. What's a white man like you been in this nigger part of town so long for? You stopped on that other street and talked to some blacks a long time and asked them about somebody named Bazemore. Now you've been down here at his house talking a long time. It don't look good. It had better not be to stir up these black people about civil rights and things like that. And you told me you raise ponies, didn't you?"

"I did."

"You been trying to sell ponies to these people? Don't you know they couldn't feed a pony when most of them can't even half feed themselves even after begging to get something for nothing out of the government? All of them put together on this street couldn't raise enough money to pay for a pony, anyhow."

"I'm not selling anything—but it is a business matter," Grover told him, becoming more irritated and provoked by the questioning. "I told you that when you asked me the first time this morning."

"Watch your talk, you. Don't you try to tell me the same thing a second time if I don't ask you."

Grover, holding back his anger, nodded without a word.

"I don't want to hear that again but there's something else I want you to tell me. Why don't you make that boy sit on the back seat? It looks like you might be trying to pass him for white but anybody can see in the daylight he's colored enough to be a nigger. You ought to know it don't look good for a nigger to be riding around town on the front seat with a white man. People don't like to see that."

"There's plenty of room up here for him. If I wanted him to sit on the back seat, I'd tell him to."

"Is that so! Now I'll tell you something. And you'd better listen good, too, because I won't be saying it but once. There's plenty of room in the jail, too, for people like you coming to town and driving around on the streets in a big automobile with a nigger sitting up on the front seat and then get careless at a traffic light or something. Instead of so much of your bigmouth talk, you'd better think about that some."

The patrol car roared away, bouncing on the rough dirt street until it went out of sight around the next corner.

Driving even more carefully than he had done earlier that morning, Grover left the Negro section of town and then went westward on the Memphis highway. Before reaching the city limit, however, he stopped first for gasoline at a filling station and then next at the drive-in Chicken Shack to get two large boxes of fried chicken for them to eat as soon as they could find a shady place to stop along the road.

Since leaving the neighborhood where Luther Bazemore lived, both of them had expected to see the patrol car again at any moment. Grover was watching the rear-view mirror and Jeff was looking in each direction at every crossing street. As it was, if the policemen had been following, they had kept out of sight.

Jeff had been moving restlessly on his side of the seat for a long time. However, he had waited until they were in open country before asking the question that Grover knew was so much on his mind.

"Mr. Grover, I want to know something."

"What is it, Jeff?"

"Mr. Grover, why didn't you leave me back there where my grandparents live?"

"Are you glad you didn't have to stay?"

"I sure am. I don't like it there. And I didn't like the way that policeman talked to you, either. We hadn't done anything wrong, had we? Why did he have to be so mean about everything?"

"That's just the way it is, Jeff. Don't let it bother you. But I'm glad you didn't have to stay, too."

"But that's why you brought me down here."

"I know. That's right. But Luther Bazemore wouldn't let you stay at his house. He didn't want you there. Your grandmother wanted you to stay—but your grandfather —I mean, Luther Bazemore—he wouldn't even listen to me about it."

"Why not?"

Looking at the highway ahead, Grover slowed down the speed of the car before answering.

"You might as well know about it right now, Jeff. You're old enough to understand and this's a good time to tell you. Your mother—Kathlee—had a white father. Not Luther Bazemore. I don't know who he was and your mother never knew, either. And you have a white father, too, just like your mother had. That makes you more white than anything else, but that's not too important. What is important is that you are my son—your mother's son—our son."

He waited until they had gone around a curve of the road before saying anything more.

"Anyway, Luther Bazemore is not really your grandfather—he's no kin to you—no more than he was kin to your mother. He knows that. And that's why he has no liking for you. It's all right for him to take pride in being black. You can understand why anybody feels proud of being what he is—black, white, or anything else. One color is no more sacred than any other color. It's a human trait everywhere to have pride in the color you were born. And you can be proud of what you are—I want you to be, Jeff. Not just because I'm your father. But because of your mother and me. What you've got to do for yourself is learn how to live as you are—you're in the middle of two worlds and neither one of them is very friendly toward you right now. One of them is Luther Bazemore's. The other one is Mike Devlin's. And it's not going to be easy living for you till there are more like you."

Realizing what had been implied, Grover glanced at Jeff. The boy had already lowered his head as if trying to hide his embarrassment.

"Never mind about that, Jeff," he said hurriedly and as kindly as he could. Reaching over, he slapped Jeff's leg in a comforting gesture. "I didn't mean to say it that way, son. Don't worry about it. I don't want you to feel ashamed about what happened. Such things can happen to anybody. And it happens all the time. I don't blame you. It was Effie Devlin's idea, anyway. And there's only one more thing I'll say about it. One of these days after you graduate from college and have learned a lot after four years of study, you'll be running the pony farm. It's going to be all yours someday—you are all I've got to pass it along to and you'll inherit it. But long before that I expect you to have your own ideas about who you want to marry and have children with. I don't care if she's black, white, or in between—just as long as she's as wonderful and beautiful as your mother was."

II

Nothing was said for the next several miles. The country was grassy on rolling hills with an occasional small poultry farm or dairy with sheds and barns close to the highway. They still had not come to a shady grove where they could stop to eat the fried chicken although trees were becoming more numerous as they went westward.

"Mr. Grover—" Jeff suddenly spoke as though he could remain silent no longer.

"What, Jeff?"

"Mr. Grover—are you ashamed of me?"

"What are you talking about?"

"My color—the way I am."

"What about it?"

"Well, I'm not white like you. And other people. And the other people don't like me for my color and—"

"That has nothing to do with the way I feel, Jeff. I like you just as you are. And I want you to remember what I said. Don't you ever think anything different about it."

"I don't want to, but—"

"Look at it this way, Jeff. Some people have black hair, some people have blond hair, some people have red hair. Does it really make any difference what the color of hair is? Of course not! So why should I be ashamed of how you look?"

"And you're really not ashamed of me?"

"I am not," he said emphatically. "Now, put that out of your mind and keep it out. Don't ever worry about that again."

Jeff had nothing more to say as he sat there looking straight ahead until presently he began squirming nervously on the seat beside Grover.

"What's the trouble, Jeff?" Grover asked kindly. "Are you still bothered about that?"

He shook his head. "It's something else. What's going to become of—happen to—to Mrs. Devlin's baby?"

"What do you mean by that?"

"Well, will we ever see him? Will I?"

Grover slowly shook his head. "I don't know, Jeff. That's something I just don't know."

"If what Mrs. Devlin said is the truth—if she was telling the real truth—"

"What about it, Jeff?"

"Well, then I sort of wish I could see him—see what he looks like."

Grover was nodding sympathetically. "I know what you

mean, Jeff. And I think I know how you feel about it. I wouldn't be surprised if someday—if they move away now—you'll want to find him and—well, you know what I'm talking about."

Jeff had turned his head and was gazing vaguely into the distance.

"It's a real strange feeling to know about that," he was saying as if talking only to himself. "I never thought about it happening to me."

"There are a lot of men in this world in the same fix, Jeff. The only difference is that some of them know they have children somewhere and others can't keep from wondering if they do—and how many."

"Mr. Grover, somehow I don't mind knowing about it. I'm glad I do. And I keep on thinking about Mrs. Devlin saying she wanted it to happen. She said it was because she didn't want to have to keep on playing with dolls any longer."

"Playing with dolls? What dolls?"

"Mrs. Devlin said she had dozens of dolls and had made a lot of them herself but playing with them made her cry because they were not real and only make-believe. She said that's why she wanted a baby."

"But if she wanted a baby so much, she's married to Mike Devlin and—"

"She said he tried but nothing happened like that and so she had to get somebody else."

"And so she selected you."

Jeff laughed a little to himself. "Well, what she said was that I was second choice because there was a white man at the stables who wouldn't do what she wanted."

"Who was that, Jeff? Was it Jim Whittaker?"

"She didn't tell me. And I was too scared to ask her anything like that."

"Well, for your information, Jeff, it wasn't me. If it had been, I'd have told her to keep on playing with her dolls and given her a dollar to buy herself another one."

"Maybe so, Mr. Grover, but Mrs. Devlin is a strong-muscled white lady and she had her muscles and mind all made up when she cornered me in the weather shelter and wouldn't pay attention to anything I said."

The highway had dipped downward to cross several hundred yards of creek-watered bottomland and on each side of the highway there was a thick growth of willows and gum trees. Grover slowed down the sedan at once and, when he saw the faint trail of a logging road into the grove, he immediately turned off the highway and followed it until they were completely shaded from the sun.

While Jeff was walking around and stretching his legs, Grover went to the stream and washed his hands and face. When he came back to the car, he was drying his face with his handkerchief.

"If anybody ever needed a shave, my face sure feels like it does," he said to Jeff. "These whiskers feel like they've been growing a week. I'd better stop in the next town and look for a barbershop. How about you, Jeff?"

Feeling his cheeks and chin, he smiled and shook his head.

"I don't feel much there right now. I've only started shaving two or three times a week and there's not much even then to shave off."

"Well, just give yourself another year or so and you'll be doing it every day. There's nothing you can do about it from then on but get up every morning and shave it off. You wouldn't want to get lazy like some people and grow a beard, would you?"

"I don't know how a beard would look but right now it wouldn't feel good on me. I'd rather stay like a boy."

Grover thought for a moment of saying something about his having already demonstrated his manhood but quickly decided it would be better not to say a word about it then.

They sat down on a grassy dry hummock and, silently and with a hungry eagerness, began eating the fried chicken from the two boxes. There were a dozen pieces of chicken in each box, legs and wings and thighs and breasts, but not a single liver or gizzard.

When Jeff had eaten the last bit he could find, he placed all the bones in a neat pile in his box before closing it.

"Mr. Grover, what happened to all the chicken livers and gizzards we didn't get?" he asked with concern. "There wasn't even a tiny little piece of them in the whole box."

"You missed them too?"

"I sure did. And they're the best parts."

"I've thought about that a lot of times. And now I've come to the conclusion that no matter where you buy chicken the people who make a big business of selling fried chicken can pick out some of the parts they like best and take them home to eat if they want to. You've seen pictures of Colonel Sanders and Minnie Pearl and Buddy Hackett begging people to buy their fried chicken and you know how happy and well fed they look. And there can be only one reason why they're so well fed. It's because they're getting all the gizzards and not sharing them with people like us. I'd rather be short-changed and short-weighted every time than have the gizzards held out. But I'll tell you what we'll do. The next time we won't buy their fried chicken if they don't promise to put in the gizzards to go with it."

"Mr. Grover, do you like gizzard sandwiches the same way I do?"

"Why wouldn't I, Jeff? It runs in the family."

"What I like to do is take a hot biscuit and open it up and spread butter on both sides of it and then put the fried gizzard in the middle to make a sandwich. I could eat a dozen of them right now."

"Me too, Jeff."

First Grover, and then Jeff, lay back on the grassy hummock in the cool shade of the gum trees. In the stillness of the afternoon there was so little breeze that there was no rustling of leaves overhead and the speeding trucks and automobiles on the highway were passing so swiftly that all of them seemed to be carrying their sound away with them.

"Where am I going to stay in Memphis, Mr. Grover?" Jeff asked as he lay there looking up at the green foliage. "I won't mind staying there all summer if they don't have policemen like those back there who talked so mean to you."

"We don't know yet where you'll stay." Grover answered sleepily. "We'll find out about that when we get there and take a good look around. I'll attend to it. Right now we need a good long nap after being up all night. I need sleep more than I do a shave—my whiskers will just have to wait. We can't go without sleep any longer."

Grover's voice was becoming more indistinct with each word he spoke. With a long, loud, drowsy yawn, he placed his hat over his face.

"We'll work out something in Memphis. . . . Don't worry, son . . . I'll take care of it. . . . Some sleep first. . . . Some sleep. . . ."

III

Jeff was the first to be awake. He sat up, rubbing his eyes and looking around him in the dark shadows of the late afternoon. The sun, barely visible through the undergrowth, was sinking into the horizon with a fiery glow and already several night birds were chirping and fluttering in the trees.

With his hat still covering his face as if he had not moved even once during all that time, Grover was sleeping soundly when Jeff got up and went down to the creek for a drink of water. When he came back, it was rapidly becoming darker under the trees with nightfall and he was glad to see Grover sitting up and looking at him. It was not often that he was afraid of being in the dark, but he imagined hearing the voices of Mike Devlin and the other men somewhere in the grove.

"I figure that was a good four-hour nap," Grover said. "And it was just about the best sleep I ever had. How do you feel, Jeff? Did you get enough sleep?"

"I feel fine now, Mr. Grover. I didn't wake up till just a little while ago right at sundown. Then I went down to the creek and got a drink of water. I thought I heard some people talking, but maybe I didn't after all."

"There might be a house somewhere near here but nobody is going to bother us—we're leaving." Grover stood up and stretched his arms. "I'm so hungry again I could eat another whole box of fried chicken. Let's get going to the next town and find something to eat."

"How do we know whose fried chicken to buy to get what we want?"

"I'll tell you. You observe the personality—and physical characteristics—of the owners of these places. For instance, when you buy a box of fried chicken from Colonel Sanders, you can count on getting the biggest thighs and drumsticks. And when you buy from Minnie Pearl, you expect to get a lot of broad-breasted white meat."

"What about Buddy Hackett's fried chicken?"

"Well, if he'd quit eating them all himself, that's when we ought to be getting the biggest gizzards of all."

"Do you want to know what I was dreaming about when I woke up a little while ago, Mr. Grover?"

"What was it?"

"We stopped somewhere to get something to eat and it wasn't fried chicken but a place where they had the biggest hamburgers I ever saw—they were this big!" He put his thumbs and forefingers together making a shape the size of a large saucer. "That's how big the hamburgers were and the buns were just as big around as that, too, and inside there was mustard and chili sauce and chopped-up onions and pickles. I never saw anything like it before. But I woke up before I could take the first bite. It sure was a fine-looking hamburger, though, even if I didn't get a taste of it before I woke up."

"You're making me hungrier than ever, Jeff. Quit talking like that and let's get going. Now I don't know whether I'd rather have a hamburger like that or a chicken gizzard sandwich. But I can eat both! Come on!"

It was only a short time after Grover had backed the sedan from the logging road and started westward again on the highway that the lights of a town suddenly appeared over the crest of a hill. It was after dark by that time and Grover knew they could not be much more than halfway to Memphis by then. At that distance, he knew it was going to be another long night and probably another sleepless one, also.

As soon as they reached the city limit, Grover stopped at the first gasoline station on the street. However, instead of getting more gasoline then, he went first to the outside telephone booth at the rear of the parking lot.

"I'm going to phone Jim Whittaker," he told Jeff as he got out of the car. "I want to find out if everything's been going along all right at the stables since we left. There might be something I ought to know about before we go any farther. Or Jim might want to ask me about something that needs to be done."

Grover was not surprised when Jim Whittaker did not answer the phone at the stable office at that time of night. However, he did answer immediately when the call was made to him at home.

"It's a good thing you called me, Grover," Jim said right away. "I didn't know how to get in touch with you and I was sitting here by the phone hoping you'd call me. Where are you now, Grover?"

"Holly Springs."

"What are you doing there?"

"I'm taking Jeff to Memphis now."

"And you didn't leave him in Tupelo?"

"No."

"Well, that's good. Now you can turn right around and bring him back here."

"Bring him back? What do you mean, Jim?"

"The boy won't be bothered now. Just listen to me, Grover, and I'll tell you why. Everything's quieted down around here and there won't be no more trouble. Those goddam night riders scattered in all directions over the country back where they came from like a bunch of scared rabbits trying to outrun a yelping old hound. They're not going to bother nobody now. Everything's been over and done with since last night. That's why you can bring the boy back to Wolverton now."

"Are you sure about this, Jim?"

"I'm as sure of it as I'm sure I'm blowing my breath in this phone. Hear that?"

"I heard it. But what happened, Jim?"

"From what I've learned listening to all the talk around Wolverton today, there was six of those goddam night riders out last night—Mike Devlin and five more. I don't know all their names right now but there was six of them altogether. I hear they stopped you on the road down south of town after you left here but didn't have enough brains among them to think to look in the trunk. That's right, ain't it?"

"That's right, Jim."

"Well, I don't want credit for it but that's exactly why I recommended putting Jeff in the trunk when you left here—I had that much confidence in them being so goddam dumb in the head they wouldn't never think about looking in there for him. Anyhow, after all that they came up this way looking for the boy. They had flashlights and looked all through the stables and barns and couldn't find him hiding nowhere and Mike kept on saying the only place they'd ever find him was hiding out in the weather shelter down by the pond. So they all went down there and set it on fire, thinking they'd either smoke him out and get him that way on the run or else burn him up inside."

"But they didn't really burn down the weather shelter, did they, Jim? Not the weather shelter—"

"They sure did, Grover. I hate to say it, but there ain't nothing left of it now but some ashes and smoldering hay. You know how much old baled hay—"

"Why did they have to do that! It's a goddam shame! The weather shelter was a special thing to me—I don't care how old and rundown it was. I wanted to keep it like that. I wanted it to stay like it's always been—I had a reason for that—"

"It's gone now, Grover, and can't be helped. But that's not all, neither. There's more to it than that. And I'll tell you about it right now. When Jeff wasn't smoked out or burned up in the fire, Mike and Bundy Godowns get into a big yelling fuss about burning down the weather shelter and destroying the property and still not finding Jeff hiding in it and Bundy cussed out Mike for doing it. Well, you know Mike and Bundy. They don't stop at nothing when

128

they get mad and cussing is only the beginning. And what that led to was some real shooting and Mike got killed."

"Mike Devlin? Dead?"

"He sure is. Dead like anybody else who's already in the cemetery with a pile of dirt over him. The way I heard it downtown in Wolverton, it was a shotgun that Bundy done it with after Mike pulled his pistol and started shooting first. And that's how it ended and why everybody there scattered in a hurry back to where they came from. Now there won't be no more trouble for Jeff like Mike started out to do. It's all over now with him gone. After what happened, nobody's going to want to take it up. The killing put an end to that. You can bring the boy on back home now."

"What about Mike's wife—Effie Devlin?"

"I'm told she took her baby and went back to Jackson today to live with her folks."

"Well, there's just one more thing I want to know."

"What's that, Grover?"

"Is my wife at home now? Have you seen Madge?"

"I haven't seen her, but I saw her red car in the driveway when I left the stables about sundown tonight. I'd say she's here now, but I wouldn't want to make a guess how long she'll stay before she goes off again. I'll tell you, if I had to put up with a contrary woman like—"

"All right, Jim. I guess that's everything for now. I'll see you in the morning. Good-by."

"Good night, Grover. And take it easy and be careful with your driving. It's a long way back here from Holly Springs in the nighttime on a strange road and it wouldn't be good to have a bad accident on the way home. I want to see you back here safe tomorrow morning."

Chapter

TWELVE

It had been a misty gray dawn that morning, and rather cool for summer too, and long after a colorless sunrise there was a lingering haze hovering over the dark green pastures and dew-damp grassy slopes of the white-fenced pony farm. Even the tall cupolas on the stables and the weather vanes on the barns and the peaked rooftop of the big white house on the ridge were only faintly visible in the smoky haze.

Once more, as it was year after year, it was the time of summer when often the day would begin with a quiet stillness as if never again would there be a breeze in the air and then in the afternoon there would be an interval of intense bright sunshine followed by a violent thunderstorm with raging winds and crashing lightning and drenching rain.

The peaceful lull in the hazy morning, however, was to be brief and abruptly ended by the piercing blast of the workday whistle at the feed mill and bagging plant in Wolverton. Then it would not be long before there would be the loud shouting of the stable boys in the paddocks, the sound of galloping hoofbeats of the frisky Shetlands in the riding ring, and the noisy clamor of a tractor mowing hay in one of the lowland fields.

In the meantime, though, all was quiet and serene in the early morning as Grover got out of his sedan after leaving it in the driveway beside Madge's car and went in an eager stride up the brick walkway to the veranda of the big white house.

After leaving Jeff at the Lawson house in Wolverton, he had hurried home hoping that Madge would be there and that she would not go away again soon. Whenever she came home after staying in Nashville for days that sometimes stretched into weeks, he was always hopeful that it was going to be the time at last when she would be considerate and loving and never leave him alone again. He wondered then if she would ever realize, or

130

care, how lonely it was for him to live in the silence of the many-roomed mansion without her.

Before opening the door to go inside, he turned and looked back at Madge's bright red convertible in the driveway. Immediately, there was a blurring of his vision as he stared at the flaming color of the car.

Ever since they were married and she had demanded that he get her a new convertible every year that was the exact same color and high-priced make, he had often tried to persuade her to let him give her a car with a different color but had never succeeded. And even though he still wanted to do anything to please her, each time he saw the familiar red color of her car he had hated the sight of it so much that he was tempted to pour a five-gallon can of gasoline over it and burn it up. He knew why he had such feelings. It had come to be a maddening symbol. The fiery red color had become firmly associated in his mind with her continual refusal to have children and a constant reminder of her habit of spending more time in Nashville than she did at home.

Even though he thought he was as much in love with Madge as ever, he often wondered how much longer he could resist the urge to make her stand and watch while he sloshed a can of gasoline on the red car and burned it up completely. And, too, there were many times when he wondered how much longer he could endure the agony of her cold indifference that was cutting deeper and deeper into him day after day from one year to the next. He had asked her many times in the past why she wanted to spend so much time away from home. However, her answers were always vague and inconclusive and, frequently, bitterly sarcastic.

And as for the mysterious and prolonged and expensive treatments which she claimed were necessary, she was always annoyed and evasive when he tried to question her about the purpose and nature of the treatments. He had long before begun to doubt that she was even telling the truth when she said she always stayed with her mother and father when she was in Nashville.

While he stood there looking at the flaming red blur, at that moment he began thinking about the way she had been treating him every time she left home. That was when she would drive off with merely a wave of her hand after blithely ignoring his asking how long she was going to be away from home and then would glance back at him with a tantalizing smile as she left him standing in the driveway with the sight of her fading away with the misty blinking of her eyes.

Leaving the veranda then and going upstairs, Grover did not want to disturb Madge's sleep that early in the morning, but he did want to have a quick glimpse of her at home after such a long time away. When he tried to open her bedroom door, though, he found it to be locked.

He was disappointed, and for several moments he was undecided about what to do, but after that he went down the hall without having knocked on her door and was careful then to make as little sound as possible while he was shaving and taking a shower. After finding a change of clothes, he went downstairs to let Annie and Della know he had come home for breakfast.

Usually when he came down to the large oak-paneled dining room in the morning, both Annie and Della were pleasantly talkative and cheerful with bright smiles on their broad black faces. Both of them took delight in finding little excuses to linger in the dining room by adjusting the curtains over the windows and smoothing imaginary wrinkles in the tablecloth and rearranging some of the dishes as if the table setting had not been properly done in the beginning.

As they busied themselves around the table, and if he did not discourage them by being too absorbed in the reading of his newspaper, they had a way of developing some slight incident into a lengthy humorously-told episode—a neighbor on their street in Halfway Hollow sweeping her front porch and finding the same dime in a crack that she had lost the week before and thought was gone forever, or a friend taking the bus to Jackson on her day off from work to go shopping and then getting on the wrong bus to come home that night and finding herself in Memphis at three o'clock in the morning.

This time, however, Annie and Della went about serving his breakfast with briskly impersonal efficiency and he could not see a trace of a smile on their faces. And instead of lingering to make a casual comment about something, which they had never failed to do before, they hurried back to the kitchen without a word each time one of them brought a dish and placed it on the table.

What was even more strange was that they said nothing about the burning of the weather shelter, which was something they certainly knew about, and, ordinarily, one of them would have made a welcoming remark when he came home after being away on a trip for a day or two. Knowing Annie and Della as he did after all those years, he decided they were disturbed about something other than the burning of the weather shelter and the reason for his having taken Jeff out of town for two nights.

Grover had finished eating his breakfast of eggs and bacon and toast and was sitting there trying to read one of the newspapers that Annie and Della had brought as usual from the newsstand in Wolverton and placed on the table for him. At the same time he was trying to think what could be the cause of the strange behavior of the two Negro women.

Della, treading softly, came from the kitchen with another pot of hot coffee.

"Thank you, Della," he said as he looked up at her impassive face. "As always, you've made real fine coffee this morning. Nobody can make coffee as good as you do, Della. You must have a coffee-making secret that nobody else knows."

Della nodded briefly without a word as if determined to hold back anything she could have said.

He continued to look up helpfully at her round, chubby face, hoping she would say something at last, but she kept her eyes averted every moment until she could leave the table and hurry from the room.

Picking up one newspaper after the other, first *The Commercial Appeal*, then *The Nashville Banner*, and finally the weekly *Wolver County Enterprise*, he tried to read the front-page headlines but actually had been seeing only some blurred print. That was when Annie, moving as silently as if she had been tiptoeing on her bare feet, came into the dining room to take away the remaining dishes.

"Annie," he spoke to her immediately, raising his voice so she could not pretend not having heard him speak to her, "Annie, I saw Miss Madge's car in the driveway when I got home a little while ago. I didn't wake her, though. I thought it was a little too early for her to have to get up. Did you see her last night when she came home?"

There was a long silence as if either she had not understood his question or was deliberately ignoring it. Finally, though, she nodded without looking directly at him.

"I saw her, Mr. Grover. And her company, too."

"She brought company with her, Annie?"

Annie made no reply.

"Who is it, Annie?"

"That's something I don't know about."

"Well, is it one of her relatives? Is it her mother or father?"

133

Her only reply was a slight motion of her shoulders.

"Well, is it anybody I know, Annie?"

Annie, backing toward the kitchen, was shaking her head. "I wouldn't think so, Mr. Grover. She didn't look to me like anybody—she didn't act like anybody you'd want to know."

"What do you mean by that?"

"That's all I know to say, Mr. Grover."

She closed her lips with disapproving tightness, although she looked as if she wanted to say more and was forcing herself to keep from being too outspoken.

"Annie, you're not telling me what I want to know."

"You'll just have to see for yourself, Mr. Grover."

She left the dining room and went back into the kitchen.

Grover picked up the coffee pot to refill his cup and, with shaking hand, sloshed coffee into the saucer and all over the tablecloth.

The hot coffee burned his lips and throat when he drank a gulp of it and then he spilled more of it on the tablecloth when he hastily put down the cup. Reaching for one of the newspapers, he tried to read while at the same time wondering why Madge's guest had made Annie and Della so disturbed. The Dow Jones stock averages, the National League baseball standings, the temperature and rainfall reports, the Mississippi River stage at Memphis, and cotton futures in New Orleans all quickly became a confused jumble of figures and percentages that were inseparable and had no meaning to him whatsoever.

II

As Grover was putting the newspaper aside, Madge came into the dining room with a tall, dark-haired woman who walked in a heavy stride and who immediately regarded him with a coldly disapproving glare as though he were an intruder who was purposely offending her by being in her presence.

Appearing to be of about the same age, Madge and the strange woman also were wearing identical clothing—flaming red shirts and pale green pants. The only thing dissimilar about them other than physical size was Madge's bright blond hair and the other woman's straggly black hair, which looked as though it had been indifferently hacked in irregular short lengths.

By the time Grover could get up from his chair, they

had already sat down side by side at the far end of the table.

"Oh!" Madge suddenly exclaimed after several moments of silence in the room as she looked across the table at Grover as though only then being aware that he was present. "This is my friend. This is Micky Pete."

Madge had turned her head and was smiling at the woman beside her.

"Micky Pete?" he repeated in surprise, looking closely at the strange woman and wondering if that could be her real name or if it had been selected to match the mannish appearance of her thick low-set eyebrows and muscular neck and shoulders. He nodded briefly. "I'm very pleased to meet you—Micky Pete."

The woman looked at him with narrowed eyes as she remained aloofly silent.

"And you! Grover Danford! You are a nasty low-down goddam son of a bitch!" Madge said in a bitterly scornful tone of voice.

Madge's face was almost colorless and her lips were thin and tight. She had drawn in her breath and she held it as long as she could while glaring at him across the table. Her upper lip suddenly began trembling.

"It won't do you any good to sit there and pretend to be deaf—you nasty bastard! Why don't you say something? You heard what I called you! And that's what you are! A nasty bastard! Did you hear that now? If you didn't—I'll keep on saying it! Bastard! Bastard! Bastard!"

"What's the matter with you, Madge?" he said after a moment, speaking as calmly as he could.

"You don't like what I called you, do you?"

"Madge, you've never talked like this before. What's happened to you? I don't know what to think of you. This is no place to talk that way. There's company here and—"

"Shut up! I'll talk as I please and where I please and when I please and you can't make me stop. You stinking slimy bastard! You're not telling me what I can't do. I do as I please. Now! Did you hear that? Grover Bastard Danford!"

He glanced at Micky Pete. She was smiling approvingly as she leaned over and nudged Madge with her arm.

"Madge! What's happened to you?" he demanded loudly, speaking out angrily. "What makes you behave like this? What's it all about?"

Closing her eyes, she laughed at him derisively with a backward tilt of her head.

135

"Grover Bastard Danford! You never had a middle name before. Now you've got one that suits you."

"Madge! What's she doing here? Who is she? What's going on between you and her? What is she?"

Madge regarded him with a contemptuous smile.

"You can't make me shut up and so you're getting mad and insulting my friend. Go ahead and keep it up and see how much good it's going to do you. And while you're about it, go on and get mad and insult both of us. All we'll do is laugh at you. You stinking slimy bastard!"

"Why do you keep on saying that, Madge?"

"Because that's what you are!"

"What makes you think that?"

"I don't have to explain anything to you."

"How long have you known her?"

"Longer than I've known you—thank God!"

"Have you been seeing her all this time in Nashville?"

"Yes! All this time! Yeh—yeh—yeh!"

"Why?"

"Yeh—yeh—yeh!"

She laughed at him again while Micky Pete was nodding encouragingly.

"Then what about these medical treatments—or whatever they were—that you said you had to have? And always told me to give you the money to pay for and wouldn't let me see the doctor's bill? What about it, Madge?"

"None of your business!"

Grover pointed his finger directly at Micky Pete.

"Have you been staying with her in Nashville every time you went there and weren't telling the truth when you said you were staying with your parents? Is that why you wanted me to promise never to phone you at their house? And never to call them, either?"

"Yeh—yeh—yeh! Not that it's any of your goddam business! Grover Bastard Danford! And we're going to keep on living together, too. And you're going to pay for it good and plenty. I'm going to make you suffer where it hurts. Oh, boy! How I'm going to make you suffer! You'll wish you'd never been born when I get through with you. Micky Pete and I are going to have the finest and biggest apartment in Nashville. Nothing but luxury. Maids day and night. Clothes. The most expensive of everything and anything you can think of. Nobody's going to have more luxury than us. I'm through living in this country slum with all those stinking stables and half-size horses of yours. Now! What do you think of that you filthy son of a bitch!"

136

"Why do you talk like this?" he asked appealingly. "What have you got against me, Madge?"

She stared at him with a tightening of her lips.

The two fiery red shirts they were wearing gradually merged into a splotch of flaming brilliance. Then all at once the flaming splotch took the shape and identical coloring of Madge's car in the driveway.

"You must know how much I've always loved you, Madge," he told her. "You couldn't keep from knowing that. And I still love you. But if this is the way you've felt about me all this time—and about her—why did you marry me? Why did you lie to me about everything? Why didn't you tell me the truth sooner?"

She smiled indifferently with a slight movement of her shoulders. Micky Pete glanced at her with an approving nod.

Grover got up from his chair. "Madge, come on with me," he ordered roughly. "I want you to go upstairs so we can talk about this in private. This is a serious matter—too serious for anybody except you and me alone."

He saw Micky Pete shaking her head as she nudged Madge with her elbow. If he had not hesitated momentarily and then held himself back, he knew he would have slapped the woman out of her chair.

"Private!" Madge said in a loud derisive outburst. "Why didn't you think of that before you made a public fool of yourself—and me, too? Private!"

He sat down again.

"What do you mean by that, Madge?"

"Why don't you try to explain it?"

"Explain what?"

Annie and Della, treading almost soundlessly, came in with the breakfast dishes for Madge and Micky Pete. Not a word was said in the room as they quickly placed the serving dishes and plates on the table and then hurried back to the kitchen. Leaning close to Madge, Micky Pete whispered to her. After that both of them, with a glance at Grover, nodded and laughed.

"You didn't answer my question, Madge," Grover spoke out in a demanding way as he looked directly at her. "What are you talking about—making a public fool of myself?"

"If you'll stop that shouting and let Micky Pete and me eat our breakfast in peace, I'll tell you. And I know plenty, too. I found out everything about you down in Wolverton yesterday—just like everybody else in this detestable little town knows all about you now and is talking

137

about you on the street. You thought you could keep it secret, didn't you, Grover Bastard Danford! Thank God, I found out about it when I did! You and that oh-so-accommodating, oh-so-beautiful, oh-so-milky-chocolate, half-white nigger bitch you used to keep! And that wavy brown-haired nigger son of yours! You nigger frigger! You nasty, dirty, slimy, stinking prick! And all this time you kept on begging me to have some of your children! Thank God, I didn't let you talk me into doing it! You nasty nigger frigger! You stinking—"

"Madge, listen to me. That was a long time ago. Long ago in the past. Years and years before I knew you—long before we were married. It has nothing to do with us."

"Like hell it doesn't! I want nothing more to do with you. You—you with that nigger son of yours with the wavy brown hair you took out of town to hide so they wouldn't kill him after he raped a white woman and she had one of your family nigger-colored babies."

"You don't know the truth about that, Madge. I don't know what you heard, but I know exactly how that happened. If you'll listen to me, I'll explain why he shouldn't be blamed for something—"

"And now you're taking up for him and trying to make excuses! Save yourself the trouble, Grover Bastard Danford. I know what everybody else in this awful little town knows about it now and I'm not going to believe your lies. I heard everything about your nigger-loving past—and present. I've never been so ashamed and humiliated in my life. To think I've been married all this time to somebody with a nigger son! And all this time you've made me be the stepmother of your nigger son! A nigger stepson! Me! It makes me so sick in my stomach I feel like throwing up in your face! Jesus Christ Almighty! Oh, how I hate you, Grover Bastard Danford! Oh, how I despise the sight of you!"

With a fling of her arm, she knocked over a drinking glass, spilling water over the tablecloth. Neither she nor Micky Pete made an effort to soak up the water with a napkin.

"And you think you're going to will him this pony farm so it'll belong to him when you're dead, don't you? And you've promised him you'll pay for all his college education, haven't you? I went downtown yesterday and heard everything—everybody in Wolverton is talking about it. God only knows what else you think you're going to do for him. Well, let me tell you something, you nigger-loving son of a bitch! Get ready for your eyes to pop open! I only married you to get all the money I could out of you —and now I'm better off than I thought I was. Now I've got the law on my side to sue you for everything you've got—your runty little ponies and everything else!"

"Madge, don't talk like this. You don't really mean it —you're excited now. Don't you remember how it was in the beginning? You knew I loved you and you couldn't have married me if money was the only—"

"You just wait and see. You'll find out. When I get through with you, there won't be a penny left for you or that half-white, half-black son of yours. He'll have to get out and sweat for a living like any nigger. And you, too. You'll have to get out and sweat for a living like the rest of them. I'm going to hire the best lawyers money can get and who'll know how to ruin you, Grover Bastard Danford. You'll suffer plenty. Oh, God, how you'll suffer! That'll pay you back for tricking me into marrying you when you were nothing but a nasty nigger frigger to start with. I wish they'd burned up that nigger son of yours when they set fire to that weather shelter the other night. I never did like the looks of that place down there and I'm glad they burned it down. Every time I saw it, it made me suspicious of what you kept it there for. Why did you? What for? For sentimental reasons? That's it. That sounds like you. It looked like the kind of place where you'd go to meet that oh-so-beautiful female of that other race."

"Shut up, Madge!" he told her roughly. "That's enough of that kind of talk. I don't want to hear any more of it."

III

Madge picked up the closest dish she could reach and threw it at Grover. He dodged in time and it crashed against the wall. Micky Pete moved another dish within her reach, but Madge was already pushing back her chair.

"Just look at him now," she said with her disdainful little laugh. "Look at him. Sitting there feeling sorry for himself. Tears ought to start any second now. He's so egotistical he thought he had such an overwhelming personality and so much devastating masculine charm that no woman could turn her back on him and walk out like I'm doing. My! How that hurts his pride! He thought I was going to spend my life having children for him—white children, for a change—while he was being a devoted father to a nigger son and raising those stupid little stunted horses of his. Oh, how he's suffering and I'm so glad!"

Turning to the other woman, Madge clasped her hand with a tight squeeze.

"Come on, Micky Pete, dear," she said with an affectionate smile, leaning over and pressing her cheek against Micky Pete's face. "Let's hurry and go home. We'll get some of my things upstairs I want to take home with us and then we can leave right away. I don't want to stay in this horrible house another minute longer than I have to. And I won't have to see it again, either, because it's going to be sold to bring in a lot of money for us."

There was a whispered comment by the lean-faced, straggly-haired woman and then, hand in hand, they left the table and started toward the doorway to the hall. Micky Pete had not spoken a word to Grover during the whole time she was in the dining room but just before passing through the doorway she glanced backward briefly and regarded him with a gloating smile of conquest. The last he saw of them was the vivid red emblem of their clothing.

Saddened and thoughtful, shivering with the first twinge of loneliness, Grover did not move from his place at the table. Even before Madge had left the house he had begun to feel the acute pain of parting and he knew it would be with him for a long time after she had gone. Having been so much in love with Madge all those years and patiently waiting for the day when she would stay at home with him and would at last be eager for them to have children of their own—and then to discover that she had turned to living with a woman like Micky Pete to gratify herself—he was doubtful now of ever again being able to trust and have complete confidence in any woman. He realized this would mean he would be living the rest of his life alone. The next moment, however, he felt a glow of happiness. There was Jeff. Kathlee's son—his son —their son.

With a determined shake of his head, he told himself that he was not going to let Madge's threat to ruin him be successful. Firmly resolved then, he was confident that Ben Dowd and as many other lawyers as necessary would be able to preserve every inch and stick of the pony farm so that someday it would be passed along to his only son. He had a lot to live for from that moment onward.

Annie and Della, undoubtedly having listened behind the kitchen door and hearing every word spoken, came into the dining room with faces beaming with delight. As

140

Annie went about sweeping the broken pieces of china into a dustpan and while Della was removing the water-soaked tablecloth, both of them unhurried and humming happily to themselves, he knew he would never have to explain why Madge was leaving him and would no longer live there.

Grover left the house through a side door and went down the sloping path to the stables without once looking back at the bright red convertible still standing in the driveway. Going directly to Governor's stall, he was sad-dling the big bay horse when Jim Whittaker walked up behind him.

"I see you got back home all right, Grover. I'm sure glad everything worked out like it did. But to tell the truth, I was plenty goddam worried there for a while. I wasn't too sure that we could get that boy away from here in the trunk of your car, but I figured at the time it was the best chance we had and I'm sure glad nothing went wrong. Just the same, I wouldn't want to have to risk it again, though. I've seen some ugly things happen in my time, but I'd say that one had the makings of the worst of all. That was a mean bunch of people after Jeff. And now that they had a quarrel among themselves—which was a good thing—and one of them got killed—which I won't comment about—anyhow, that ought to learn them a lesson and scatter them for good and keep them from ganging up like that again."

Stroking Governor's silky neck, Grover nodded but said nothing. The horse, lowering his head, nuzzled Grover's chest and excitedly stomped his hoofs several times.

Grover was thinking about Madge and Micky Pete and he was hoping that Jim would make no comment about Madge's convertible being in the driveway. He wanted to wait until some other time before telling him what had taken place in the dining room that morning.

"The only trouble about the whole thing now is that the weather shelter down there by the pond got burned up," Jim was saying. "I sort of miss seeing it down there after all these years where it'd come to be a personal kind of landmark you never want to lose sight of and somehow I can't get used to it being all gone now and only some ashes to show for it and even that will blow away when the next strong wind comes along. I looked down there in the meadow a while ago where the shelter used to be and I tell you I got a real sad feeling inside me about it. Most things I can take like they come when they're bound to happen, but that's not one of them. I got to thinking all

141

about how the young ponies used to hightail it to that weather shelter when a fast-moving thunderstorm came up and how they made a fine excuse of it to crowd in there close together and jostle one another like some young children squealing playfully and hiding under the bed from the thunder and lightning. That's how it always was with the colts and it sure was a sight to see."

Jim patted Governor on the rump and the big old horse pawed the ground and switched his tail as if eager to leave the stable and gallop away.

"That's one feeling I've got about losing that shelter, Grover. Another is like having a great big old oak tree in the front yard of your house that you've been used to seeing as long as you can remember in your life and then wake up some morning to find that a windstorm came along in the night while you slept and uprooted it and the fine green leaves are already shriveled up some and you hate to know it won't never be standing there no more to make the cool shade in your yard in the hot summer sun. I reckon I can't keep from being sort of softhearted about some things in this life, after all."

"It's not going to be like that, Jim."

"What do you mean? The weather shelter's gone. It just ain't there now. You can go and see for yourself."

"I'm going to ride down there and take a good look and while I'm gone I want you to get busy and hire the carpenters right away and send for the lumber we need. We're going to build that weather shelter right back in the same place like it's always been and waste no time about it."

It was a moment before Jim could say anything.

"Grover—do you really mean that?" he asked then.

"I sure do."

A broad smile came to Jim's face.

"And I'm sure glad to hear you say you want to do that, Grover. It would never seem like the same place around here to me without it. When you've got a special personal reason like I have—"

"What reason is that, Jim?"

"Well, I never mentioned it to you before, because it's more personal than anything else, but when I was a young man working for your daddy—"

He stopped abruptly, his eyes blinking, and slowly drew the palm of his hand over his weather-browned cheeks and chin. His expression brightened then as if he had wiped years of age from his face.

"Well, like I said, when I was a young man, that

142

weather shelter was the special place where I took my wife to court her every Sunday afternoon so I could persuade her to get married to me. When you grow older like it is with me now and think back about some things long ago—Sunday afternoons in the summertime and those frisky colts and that sweet tingling smell of new-crop hay in the weather shelter and the female courting you've been anxious for all week to do so much you can hardly wait—"

Grover turned and looked away.

"I know what you mean, Jim."

"Grover, I reckon you've got the same kind of human feelings I've got for things."

"It goes down real deep inside, doesn't it, Jim?"

"Goddam it, it sure does, Grover. It sure does."

Outstanding Fiction Available in SIGNET Editions

☐ **MOTHERS AND DAUGHTERS by Evan Hunter.** From the author of **Strangers When We Meet** comes a compelling story of four women of different ages and temperaments, whose lives are closely linked by the threads of love. (#Y3855—$1.25)

☐ **AN ORDERLY LIFE by Jose Yglesias.** The story of the "sweet smell of success," one man's rise from the cigar center in Tampa to a big office on Madison Avenue and a home in the suburbs. (#Q3973—95¢)

☐ **THE LOCKWOOD CONCERN by John O'Hara.** A national bestseller, the century-spanning saga of a family in pursuit of money, power, status, and sex, set in the "O'Hara" country of eastern Pennsylvania. (#Y3779—$1.25)

☐ **THE GROUP by Mary McCarthy.** One of the most talked-about novels of recent years, this is the daring and brilliant story of eight Vassar graduates trying to cope with life and love during the turbulent depression years. A United Artists movie release. (#Q2501—95¢)

☐ **HURRY SUNDOWN by K. B. Gilden.** The sensational bestselling novel in which a group of intensely human characters become involved in every kind of conflict when the rival forces of tradition and progress make a battlefield of their Southern community. (#W2860—$1.50)